THE
ENGLISH
EXPERIENCE

Julie Schumacher

DOUBLEDAY

New York

This is a work of fiction. Names, characters, places, and incidents either are the product of the author's imagination or are used fictitiously. Any resemblance to actual persons, living or dead, events, or locales is entirely coincidental.

Copyright © 2023 by Julie Schumacher

All rights reserved. Published in the United States by Doubleday, a division of Penguin Random House LLC, New York, and distributed in Canada by Penguin Random House Canada Limited, Toronto.

www.doubleday.com

DOUBLEDAY and the portrayal of an anchor with a dolphin are registered trademarks of Penguin Random House LLC.

Interior illustration credits: page 19: illustration by Dan Bruggeman, photo by Block Portrait Studios | page 189: Album / Alamy Stock Photo | page 190: illustration by Dan Bruggeman, photo by Block Portrait Studios | page 191: image based on an Alamy stock photo

Jacket illustration (umbrella) by Evan Sklar, based on a photograph by Jupiterimages/Polka Dot/Getty Images
Jacket design by Emily Mahon
Book design by Betty Lew

Library of Congress Cataloging-in-Publication Data
Names: Schumacher, Julie, 1958– author.
Title: The English experience : a novel / Julie Schumacher.
Description: First Edition. | New York : Doubleday, [2023]
Identifiers: LCCN 2022056597 | ISBN 9780385550123 (hardcover) |
ISBN 9780385550130 (ebook)
Classification: LCC PS3569.C5548 E64 2023 | DDC 813/.54—dc23
LC record available at https://lccn.loc.gov/2022056597

MANUFACTURED IN THE UNITED STATES OF AMERICA

1 3 5 7 9 10 8 6 4 2

First Edition

For Winifred and Frederick Schumacher

(Mom, I don't think you would have approved of Jay Fitger,
but Dad might have liked him.)

ONE

Jason Fitger, chair of the Department of English at Payne University, found himself summoned, in mid-December, to the office of the new provost. The job of provosts was to create and then disseminate bad news, so he expected her to announce a new punitive measure to be inflicted on his academic unit, which had scarcely survived the crises of the previous years. Instead, after arranging her features into a facsimile of cordial goodwill, she claimed to be presenting him with an opportunity, "truly a plum."

Fitger braced himself, preparing to hear it.

"You're probably familiar with our 'Experience: Abroad' programs," the provost said.

Yes, he was familiar with them. He had in fact argued against their existence, first because of the shortage of faculty willing and able to teach internationally, and second because of the absurd and gratuitous colon between the words "experience" and "abroad."

The provost, adhering to the serpentine rhetorical style of the university's upper administration, offered some prefatory remarks about the challenging times Payne had endured, and about the tenacity and community spirit that had allowed the university, a shining beacon of higher learning, to prevail.

Fitger retied a shoelace and waited.

"I'm inviting you to teach the Experience: England class this coming January term in London," she said, leaning back in her leather chair.

The January term at Payne began in less than three weeks, and Fitger hadn't yet graded his essays from the fall. He told the provost he wasn't interested.

She seemed not to have heard him. Like all the Experience: Abroad classes, the England seminar, she explained, was interdisciplinary in nature, involving cultural studies, art, religion, history, government, and, of course, literature—but, once he took the course over for himself, he would be free to tweak the curriculum if he chose. The program was based in a lovely neighborhood on the fringes of London, with day trips to Oxford, Stonehenge, and Bath. If she were able to make the trip herself, she would jump at the chance. This was, in essence, a three-week salaried vacation, not to mention an escape from Payne and its weather during the worst of the winter. She certainly envied him.

"There's no need for envy; I'm not available," Fitger said.

Really? What made him say that? The provost smiled.

What made him say it? Well, it was true. First, there were various university tasks, most of which had their origin in her office, that he had to take care of; and there were spring semester classes to prepare; and, theoretically, a few meager days for his own vacation, sure to be punctuated by as-yet-unforeseen emergencies that invariably cropped up over the course of any holiday. Besides: Were department chairs, with their Kafkaesque workloads, truly the best candidates for—

The provost waved these objections away. Easy enough to bring his departmental tasks with him. He could probably take care of them on the plane. It was almost 2013, and there was a little invention he might have heard of; it was called the personal computer . . . She leaned toward him over the immaculate expanse of her desk, and Fitger was reminded of a python flexing its coils in preparation for an assault on its prey. She wasn't talking about sending him to Cedar Rapids, for god's sake. This was London. Theaters, museums, the changing of the guard, high tea with scones and jam, the queen . . . Everyone loved London.

Jason Fitger did not love London. The last time he'd been there was at least a decade earlier with his then wife, Janet, and his primary memories of the trip involved a sodden cylinder of blood pudding, an evening of poorly timed sex, and rain. Surely there were anglophiles somewhere on the Payne campus, members of the faculty endowed with resources beyond a vague hostility to all things British, who might be willing—if not eager—to teach such a class. What about Ravenel, in Theater?

No. The provost had already asked her.

Sheffield, in Sociology?

Also a no.

Ruiz? Allington?

No and no. Ideally, the course would be taught by the faculty member who had proposed it: Randy Lortimer, in History. "But . . ." The provost paused. "There were . . . complications."

3

Complications, as Fitger and everyone else on the Payne campus knew, involved Lortimer being removed from his office in a straitjacket the week before—probably driven around the bend by the paperwork and regulations associated with taking a group of undergrads abroad.

The provost looked at her watch. The students had paid their fees, she said. The tickets were purchased, the housing and schedule and coursework arranged. To be blunt: Payne wasn't prepared to refund or lose the money. And what else did he have to do over the winter break? While the other faculty she had approached had family and holiday commitments, Fitger (she happened to know) was childless and divorced and, in curmudgeonly fashion, had long lived alone.

Perhaps more to the point: She would be reviewing his department's budget request at the end of next month. How did he feel about the possibility of receiving—or never again receiving—assistance or protection of any kind from her office?

Fitger took a deep breath and looked down at the carpet. Near his left foot, some sort of insect—a variety of ant or small beetle—was traversing the thread-like fibers, plunging down to the polyester forest floor and laboriously scrambling up again. "Does this class have a syllabus?" he asked.

Of course it did. Every class at Payne had a syllabus. The provost would have her assistant send it to him, along with a packet of information, including profiles of the students, all of whom had been carefully vetted. Travel and other logistics had all been arranged. Was his passport current? Good; it was settled.

They stood. On the flat of the desk between them, Fitger saw a slip of paper with a list of names, all of them crossed out except for his own, at the bottom. The provost wished him a pleasant trip.

Fitger was, as per the provost's description, childless and divorced, but he didn't live entirely alone. He and his ex-wife, Janet Matthias, co-owned a dog, trading him back and forth like a surly intermediary between their two homes. A mutt of uncertain lineage, Rogaine was a threadbare, unappealing creature; Fitger had misgivings about his character and disposition and suspected that Rogaine's feelings toward him were the same.

Now, sitting in Janet's kitchen with a worn leash dangling from his hand, Fitger explained that, due to the provost's opinion of him as a friendless recluse, he would be unavailable for canine care for three weeks—from January first to the start of spring term. "What are you making, by the way?" he asked. The room smelled of onions and garlic.

"Vegetarian goulash. With a side of poached chicken for Rogaine." Janet wiped her hands on her apron and, plucking a pen from a container that was labeled PENS, she consulted the large paper calendar on her closet door. A paper calendar, Fitger thought, was a lovely nostalgic touch in a kitchen. On Janet's version, the dog-custody days were clearly marked. He watched her revise her January schedule.

"Hm." She frowned. "He's got a veterinary appointment on the fifteenth. I took him last time, so this one's your turn."

Fitger looked at the dog, sitting between them on the

tile floor and licking its genitals. "I suppose we could trade. Would you be able to—"

"No. No trading. I'll call and reschedule him," Janet said. "So you can take him when you get back. He's supposed to have his teeth cleaned. And he needs his shots. He should also have his anal sacs milked."

"Excuse me?"

"Don't pretend you don't know about it," she said. "That's why he scoots his ass along the rug."

"Intriguing. Soup to nuts it is, then," Fitger said. He hated taking the dog to the vet. Normally a brazen, hubristic beast, Rogaine behaved like a demented coward as soon as they walked through the door. He thought about asking Janet to be more flexible in regard to this taking-of-turns but remembered that inflexibility was one of his ex-wife's more dependable traits.

"It was fairly insulting, the way I was asked to teach the class." He poked the dog's left hindquarter with his toe, and Rogaine responded with a half-hearted snarl. "As if I were the last person on campus to be considered."

Janet opened her refrigerator and burrowed through the crisper drawers. "You probably *were* the last person."

"I do have thirty years of teaching experience," he said, directing his comments to the back of her neck.

She turned around, an odd-looking vegetable in her fist. "And you think that's a qualification?"

"What do you mean?" Fitger was distracted by the vegetable, a sort of well-coiffed cauliflower that appeared to be ready for a night on the town. "Why wouldn't it be a qualification?"

"Because—" She tossed the vegetable into the sink. "Teaching abroad is totally different from teaching on campus. You're hardly nurturing."

"I need to be nurturing?"

"You'll be with the students all day," she said. "You don't typically *like* students. And you're a difficult person. You don't know how to have conversations. I'm sure I've said this before: You're not well socialized. You lack personal skills."

"That's a flattering little sketch." He watched her savage the odd-looking vegetable with a knife. "What on earth is that thing you're dissecting?"

"Romanesco. You don't even relate to the dog very well."

"The dog has a damaged personality," Fitger said. "He has a romantic attachment to the arm of my couch. And you know I hate the word 'relatable.'"

Janet pointed out that she had used the word "relate" and not "relatable"—and there were plenty of words that, for reasons of his own which she didn't want to hear him explain, he seemed to dislike. She lobbed the pieces of vegetable into the pot on the stove and turned toward him. "Jay: You don't like England. And you're a terrible traveler. Why would you agree to teach a class about traveling in England?"

"Well, the focus isn't specifically 'travel.' I'm not sure what it is. Why do you say I'm a terrible traveler?"

"I won't even bother to answer that," Janet said. "You're sixty-three years old. You've been teaching the same four or five classes for the past twenty years, and you usually dedicate your January term to lying on the couch, complaining that you don't have time to get your writing done."

7

This seemed unfair. Of course he was short on time: he was chairing a department. And why had she referenced his age? She was obviously getting older, too—though he had to admit that her regular tennis games, as well as a recent, somewhat annoying interest in wellness, appeared to keep her in very good shape. "I don't think you appreciate how much work is involved with running an academic unit. You haven't had the—"

"Oh, sweetheart," Janet said.

Fitger startled: his ex-wife didn't care for endearments or sentimentality. During the early years of their marriage, he had given her an anniversary card and found it ten minutes later, torn in half, in the trash. But she was talking not to him but to Rogaine, who was butting the backs of her knees with his rocklike skull. Fitger watched as she lowered her face toward the dog's. "Are you asking for a snack before you go? Is that what you want?"

"A snack is always welcome," Fitger said, speaking for himself as well as the dog. "We're not in a rush, though. That smells very good, by the way. That vegetable stew . . . with or without chicken."

Janet ignored him and returned to the stove, both Fitger and Rogaine observing her closely, competing suitors temporarily aligned.

Because Janet enjoyed gossip about the higher-ups at Payne, Fitger told her about his meeting with the new provost in more lurid detail, describing the bloodred color of her fingernails and the oversized photo of the Payne mascot, a prairie dog with miniature forelimbs, that occupied one of her office walls. He shared his hope that, due to his willingness to serve as an academic chaperone in England, the administration would be indebted to English. "We need to hire new faculty, and if I could manage to—"

"I've applied for a new job," Janet said.

"What?" Fitger's ex was a senior administrator at the Payne University law school. He watched her rinse out a dark blue ceramic bowl. Compared to the dented metal dish he used at Fitger's, the dog enjoyed much nicer dinnerware here. "What sort of job?"

She turned toward him, brandishing a paring knife like a weapon. "This is *confidential,* Jay. I haven't told anyone at work."

"My lips are sealed," he said. "Is this about money? You need a raise?"

"Why would that be the first thing you think of?"

"Why wouldn't it be?" he asked. "You deserve a raise. And a better title. If you'd argued for a better title a few years ago, which I remember telling you to do, you'd be in a stronger position to bargain for—"

"Jay? Forget it. Forget I mentioned it. The topic is closed." She set the bowl of sliced chicken on the floor for the dog; the meat was gone in three seconds.

Fitger decided not to question her further. Janet was known for a bit of a temper: during one of the low points in their marriage, when she was angry with him about something, she had nailed one of his shirts to the closet door with a staple gun. He had worn it with holes in the sleeves until it disappeared from his wardrobe. He changed the subject.

"It must be more than a dozen years since you and I were in England. Do you remember that horrid hotel room we had in London? That sooty little place with the shared bath?"

"I've worked hard to erase that entire trip from my memory," Janet said.

"Understandable." Fitger nodded. "We had that flat tire in the middle of nowhere in the Wessex Downs. And there was the unfortunate afternoon—no one's fault, of course—with the roadside sheep. But we weren't miserable the entire time, were we? The Cotswolds were pleasant, I think."

"I believe the word you used to describe our weekend in the Cotswolds was 'harrowing.'" Janet filled the dog's water bowl and watched him drink. "We nearly killed each other in a town called Lower Slaughter. And there was that problem with the laxatives you thought were aspirin."

"Yes, I'd forgotten about that," Fitger murmured. Rogaine looked back and forth between them. Fitger often had the impression that the dog was privately evaluating and critiquing their discussions. "Why did we choose England?" he asked. "Ten or fifteen years back, or whenever it was— why didn't we go to Provence or Norway or Greece, for god's sake?"

"We went to England," Janet said, pulling a bottle of red wine from a rack above the sink, "because you promised that if you sold your novel we would take a trip; we'd go to Europe. But once you sold it, the advance was smaller than you thought it should be, so instead of celebrating you decided to sulk, and by the time you pulled your head out of your ass the fares had gone up, and England was the only place we could afford."

Fitger had to admire her level of recall: she demonstrated a particular gift for recollection when it came to his blunders and miscalculations, each of which had served as a grain of sand in the hourglass of their divorce. "Well, we should have gone to Greece," he said. "But of course it's never too late. One day you might—"

"I did go to Greece, actually. A few weeks after the divorce. I went by myself." She pulled the cork from the bottle. "Ten days on Crete. It was glorious—a perfect vacation."

"Hmm." He watched her inhale the wine's scent. She closed her eyes, perhaps indulging in visions of whitewashed sunshine, azure water, and the sinewy arms of a libidinous Greek millionaire.

She set the bottle and a half dozen glasses on the counter and looked at the clock. "Okay, it's time for you to get out of here. Goodbye. My tennis group will be here at six."

Janet was a member of many groups. Fitger didn't bother to ask her why a tennis group would be gathering for a vegetarian repast rather than for tennis: this was just the sort of question that his ex-wife disliked.

"You'll bring him back tomorrow afternoon?" she asked, looking fondly at the dog.

Fitger nodded and clipped the leash to the animal's collar, then put on his gloves and coat and hat. It was nearly a two-mile walk between his house and Janet's.

She asked him if he had a poop bag. No, he did not. He often forgot them. She gave him one.

"How many students are you taking with you?" she asked. "Have you met them?"

"Eleven. And, no. I'm sure they've all gone home by now for

the break. But I have a file of their letters and applications—everything from fingerprints to DNA tests."

Janet opened the door. Winter was a long and demanding season at Payne, with one variety of snow on top of another. The yellow light of her kitchen spilled onto the walk. Fitger felt like a soon-to-be exile, about to be shipped off to the tundra without his ration of vegetable stew.

"At least it's just winter term and not a full semester," he said, as Rogaine tugged at the leash. "What can happen in three weeks?"

"I don't know," Janet said. "But I guess you'll find out."

TWO

FELICITY BABINEC STATEMENT OF INTEREST

Dear Experience: Abroad Office,

My name is Felicity Babinec and I am applying for the Experience: England program with Professor Lortimer in January. I took Survey of American History with Professor Lortimer last year and enjoyed it a lot. He did a magic show to make a point about the War of 1812 that was not like anything in a classroom I ever saw.

At Payne I am majoring in Elementary Education (Kindergarden or first grade.) My interest in England is that it is a place where a lot of poets are from. I love to write poems and sometimes I read them too when I have the time.

Although I have never been out of the US I am eager to set my foot in foreign lands. Seeing and understanding other cultures will be important to my teaching career. My personality is shy but I am easy to get along with, I think, that is one of my strengths. One of my weaknesses is, I am not as brave as I should be (I will be nervous when the plane takes off!) but that is something I am working on.

Thanks!

One final word about me
is that
I have never been away
from Mrs. Gray—
she is my cat.

SONIA MORALES—ADDENDUM
TO STUDENT APPLICATION

To the person reading this who it might concern,

I want to withdraw my application to the Experience: England class if Brent Schraft is one of the other students. Brent and I applied together but it was my original idea and when we sent the paperwork in (I got a scholarship and Brent didn't, that is a whole nother story) we were still a couple but now we are broken up.

To be honest I think Brent should withdraw, he is not the one with the scholarship and like I already said this was not his plan it was mine. Plus the fact that it is his fault that we broke up, I was not the one who hooked up with that girl with one leg from our Chem 101. Brent says it didn't mean anything and he did it because she was a better student than both of us. Which translates to say that his f***ing her was more than one kind of cheating, because he cheated against me and also cheated so he could bring up his grade.

That is not something I can respect.

The scholarship office says I can't have the money back if I don't go on the trip but that is not true for Brent because he didn't get any scholarships. I don't think that's fair.

I hope you will take his name off the list.

JOSEPH (JOE) BALLO: OPTIONAL PERSONAL
STATEMENT/DISCLOSURE—CRIMINAL RECORD

To the Instructor.

I am not sure whether you have seen my full records. When I applied to college they were all included but they may not be now. If you have seen the full records you are aware of my Disclosure of Criminal Activity.

This is what you should know. I have had the opportunity to apply for my record to be expunged as one of my lawyers recommend. This would be a permanent sealing or destroying of my criminal record which is related to an act which occurred when I was fourteen. It ended with my spending eighteen months in a juvenile rehabilitation facility. But I have chosen not to expunge. My record is my record. I will not pretend that it doesn't exist.

I am ashamed of what I did (it was an accident) but not who I am.

P.S. For reasons that are obvious in the records and in my disclosure I am claustrophobic. I also sometimes walk in my sleep.

WYATT FRANKLIN STATEMENT OF INTEREST

Hey, my name is Wyatt Franklin and I am totally psyched about our January trip to the Cayman Islands. Anthropology is not my major but if it's "the science of what makes us human" then I am on board.

What I look forward to most is the stingray city and the blue iguanas. I know we will be digging stuff up during the heat of the day but I will be ready (I will bring sunscreen, last 4th of July I burned my skin so bad it flaked off in chunks). I have snorkeling experience, but only in Florida and it wasn't that good. I have never snorkeled in a bioluminescent bay like the one in Cayman and never in turquoise water near a sunken ship. Please let me know if I will need my own snorkeling gear.

Here are a couple of things about me. I am a junior majoring in Health Sciences. I was originally doing pre-med but my GPA last year had a different idea. Last summer I completed a Wilderness First Responder course so I am licensed for search and rescue, joint dislocations, and airway and wound management. I also used to play jazz clarinet.

I sometimes suffer from depression especially during the winter months when the dark and cold make me feel like I am being sucked every day down a bottomless well. But that won't be a problem at Grand Cayman! 😎

TEN REASONS WHY ANDROMEDA AND CASSIOPEIA WAGNER-HALL ARE APPLYING FOR THE "EXPERIENCE: ENGLAND" CLASS

1) The Royal Academy of Arts
   We are both art majors—studio as well as art history. Is there a better place to study art than London? Short answer: no.
2) The Victoria and Albert
   We may not have mentioned up to now that we are twins (identical)—hence our joint statement and application. We are both studying under Prof. Wayetu (Studio Art—best prof at Payne by far, her print-making class is a mind-altering experience). Wayetu says we have to go to the V & A and Wayetu is our personal goddess so to the V & A we will go.
3) The Tate Modern
   Warhol (Marilyn) vs. Picasso (the Weeping Woman)—though we note the traditional objectification of women by male artists.
4) The Courtauld
   Okay, the impressionists, and especially Berthe Morisot. "A bunch of lunatics and a woman." Hahahaha.
5) Brick Lane/Brick Lane Gallery
   Banksy Banksy Banksy Banksy Banksy Banksy Banksy Banksy Banksy Banksy Banksy
6) The Tate Britain
   Because Professor Wayetu told us to look for the Gwen John self-portrait. Gwen John, at a Cezanne exhibit, said Cezanne's paintings were good, "but I prefer my own." *Kick-*

ass! Note to the art department: don't let Wayetu go on leave until after we graduate next year.

7) Leighton House

We just found this online. OMG Islamic tiles.

8) The Freud Museum—because our mother is a psychoanalyst who actually has a photo of Sigmund Freud, with his pointy beard and his phallic cigar and neurotic watch chain, in her office. She has already mentioned this museum five or six times and would probably put us up for belated adoption if we didn't send her a photo of the famous couch.

9) Sir John Soane's Museum

Dude had a sarcophagus in his living room.

10) The National Portrait Gallery

Because the goddess Wayetu wants us to "understand faces." These two are ours:

BRENT SCHRAFT

Begin your letter with an appropriate professional Dear Payne Experience Abroad Office,

I am applying for the January in London. It will definitely be an experience I will be benefitting from. Now and in the future.

My career reasons *List your career goals as well as academic reasons for* applying for this trip are about Improving. My chances for one day starting a worth-while career. My academic reasons are the same. Wanting to experience things I have not heard of or seen. I applied for London England with a friend.

Include any specific interest you may have in the local culture or history of the

England is apart of the British Kingdom. Rugby and soccer are common there. I will be following the NBA games especially the Wisconsin Buck and the Bulls. My Dad saw Michael Jordan before the second time, in '98 he retired.

Your major is math. I have an accentuating circumstance, that is I struggle with writing I am not good with words. It is not I am sluffing things off, we can't all be good at the same thing. My transcript says I was on probation which it is not true. That was a course in Sociology I had a D in, I told the prof my problems with writing she didn't give me a chance. I am better at math. I am hoping we will not be writing during this class.

Include any other relevant If you put us in groups I would like to be in the one with Sonia Morales.

Yours sincerely, Your Name

ELWYN YANG STATEMENT OF INTEREST

Ivy-encrusted headstones. Wraiths. Dungeons and crooked alleyways echoing with the tormented screams of the damned. London overflows with haunted places, most of which I intend to see during our three-week tour.

Allow me to introduce myself. My name is *Elwyn P. Yang*, and I am a sophomore with a solid academic reputation and a personal interest in horror (H.P. Lovecraft) and the occult. In preparation for our trip I have read several books about Jack the Ripper. If the Jack the Ripper tour is not on our schedule I will add it for myself.

I have not seen a copy of our itinerary but I assume it will include the Tower of London. May I suggest we also visit the Old Operating Theatre Museum (soundproof because they didn't use anesthesia), Epping Forest which is well known as a hideaway used by murderers, and the historic cemeteries, especially the pet burying ground in Hyde Park. I will bring information about each of these to share.

To answer the question about my ability to cooperate and get along with a group, I will say that I am not particularly "well liked." I am a business major (3.6 GPA) for the obvious reasons. There are no jobs out there for people who just want to read.

I do not have any allergies and don't take medications except for a topical steroid in case my eczema (it is not contagious) gets out of hand.

XANNA BLYTHE OPTIONAL
PERSONAL STATEMENT/DISCLOSURE

"Are there other relevant aspects of your personal or academic background you would like to disclose?" I guess that depends on what 'relevant' means. **I've got ADD**—but who doesn't? Paying attention for more than ten minutes at a time is a thing of the past. **I go to therapy every Thursday.** Dr. Markov, all-campus shrink (what kind of campus has only one shrink?), is willing to be in touch if I need it. I asked if he'd miss me while I was gone, and he tipped his head back and showed me the underside of his beard.

I guess I could list my status as a **procrastinator and underachiever**. You'd want to talk to my high school guidance counselor, Ms. Forster, about this one; I think I broke her spirit when I told her the only college that accepted me was Payne.

I haven't seen anything about cell phone policy during this trip but I should probably disclose here that I have a **Concerned Parent** (hi, mom!) who likes to be in touch on a regular basis, that is, about every eight minutes. I tell her not to worry about me but she likes to remind me that she spent twenty-two hours pushing me out of her birth canal, and that gives her the right. She will probably call 911 and the US Air Force and the wildlife hotline if I don't answer my phone.

Occasional nihilism.

Also **an auto-immune disease,** mostly controlled, but we don't have to talk about that because like I said, it's mostly controlled.

Onward,

X. Bythe

LIN JEN SNOW STATEMENT OF INTEREST

I signed up for this trip because my government/pre-law major requires study abroad which has historically been about young white Americans losing their virginity and learning how to use the salad fork. Tourism is a consumerist industry that wastes resources, contributes to climate crisis, and reinforces colonialist tropes. If Payne isn't going to fund these trips (I already have $38,000 in loans) they shouldn't require us to do them.

I am not interested in British "culture." I don't care what kind of hats the royal family members are wearing and I'm not going to eat the fish and chips (I am a vegan).

If I can afford law school after Payne I intend to work on immigration reform.

D. B. MELNYK: STUDENT APPLICATION, "EXPERIENCE: ABROAD"

THREE

Wearing a large cardboard nametag on a string around his neck like a child on an orphan train, Fitger met his students at the airport and checked their names off his list. Here were the provost's carefully vetted undergrads, among them a claustrophobe from a juvenile detention center; a student who erroneously believed he was headed for the Caribbean; a pair of unreconciled lovers; a set of undifferentiated twins; and one person who had never been away from her cat before.

One young woman arrived belatedly at the check-in with a set of matching metal lockers on wheels. "I wanted to get here earlier," she said. "But I packed and unpacked at the last minute. I had trouble deciding what to bring. And my travel iron takes up a lot of room." She pointed to her name on his list. "I'm Sonia Morales."

Fitger made a tick mark at the edge of his list: *S for Suitcases = Sonia.* Each year he found it more and more challenging to learn students' names. He had taught so many of them, and in recent years they'd begun to strike him as alarmingly young. He had already assigned mnemonics to *B for Basketball Fanatic = Brent* (wearing a Chicago Bulls sweatshirt); to *F for Feline-Loving Felicity* (wearing a T-shirt with an image of her cat); and to *L for Litigator = Lin*. Lin was the pre-law/government student. Having seen her wear away the resistance of a check-in attendant regarding an expired voucher for an airline meal, Fitger made a mental note: if he was in trouble with the law in ten years, he would know whom to call.

He helped *S for Suitcases = Sonia* with her luggage, recalling the recommended packing list and its suggestions about traveling light. "You brought an iron with you?" he asked. "For ironing clothes?"

"Yeah." She hefted the first of the lockers onto the scale. "I figure this trip is going to be stressful, and ironing always helps me relax."

They cleared security with only one mishap involving a taser and a quart of milk (the same student), both tucked at the bottom of a carry-on bag, and made their way to the gate. Some of the students sprawled across the vinyl seats with their belongings; others scavenged for last-minute provisions: chips and magazines and electronics and inflatable toilet-seat-shaped pillows. *J for Juvenile Detention = Joe* explained to Fitger that, due to his aversion to enclosed spaces, he would not be drinking anything or making use of the airline bathroom during the flight.

"Good to know," Fitger said.

W for Wrong Way = Wyatt tossed his Caribbean guidebook into the trash and said he hoped the weather would be decent in England, while Sonia, examining her boarding pass, said she needed someone to trade seats with her; she wasn't going to spend seven hours staring at the side of Brent Schraft's head.

One of the students asked for a copy of the course syllabus; Fitger handed one over as they boarded the plane.

This turned out to be a mistake. About twenty minutes after takeoff, *L for Litigator = Lin* stood in the aisle of the plane beside him, tapping his shoulder. He'd already kicked off his shoes and reclined and put on his sleeping mask. "I have a question," she said, when he propped himself upright and took off his mask. "Why is this class totally different from the one we signed up for?"

"It's not totally different." Fitger groped around the floor for his shoes. "We're still going to England."

"Right," Lin said. "But this was supposed to be a history class. It was taught through the History Department. I don't see anything about history or government here."

Fitger resisted the temptation to say that what Lin had signed up for was a series of whimsical notions rather than a class: Lortimer's syllabus, sent only at Fitger's repeated insistence a few days before, was a deranged and very rough draft. He explained that all of Payne's Experience: Abroad classes were designed to cross, rather than reside within, disciplines. But, yes, given the last-minute substitution of one professor for another, some alterations to the curriculum had occurred.

Lin nodded—not, it seemed, to show that she agreed with this statement, but as if confirming that her suspicions about Fitger and his class were correct. She stood in the aisle while he remained seated, which seemed to reverse, in an unfortunate way, the traditional student-teacher dynamic. She flipped to the third page of the syllabus. "You have us writing a paper every day."

"Yes." He felt like a witness addressing a jury.

"*Every day*," she said. "With a longer essay due at the end. Doesn't that seem like a lot?"

"All but the last of these are very short essays," Fitger said. "They're more like responses than full-blown papers. And this is the only class you're currently enrolled in, so—"

"The thing is," Lin said, "I asked around, and everyone I've talked to thinks that having a paper due every day is kind of unreasonable."

"You've already caucused?" Fitger struggled to turn toward her, but his seatbelt seemed to have tightened of its own volition. In the center segment of his row, several human beings were climbing under and over one another, and one of them was kneeling on the end of Fitger's belt. "Uhouff," he said.

"Oops. Did I hurt you?" *F for Feline = Felicity,* clutching a backpack and blanket and pillow, had overtaken the seat to his right. "I wanted to sit next to someone from our trip," she said, "and that lady said she would trade with me. I don't really care about having a seat by the aisle." Did Professor Fitger want to see some photos of Felicity's cat, Mrs. Gray? Look: here she was playing with a catnip mouse. Mrs. Gray had never seen a real mouse because she was an indoor cat, but a couple of years ago, or it might have been last year, a bird had flown through their front door, and Mrs. Gray had chased it into the bathroom, and if Felicity's mother hadn't rushed in to open the window—

In the aisle to his left, Lin tapped him on the shoulder again. She had assembled a small group of co-complainants.

In regard to the reading but particularly the writing assignments, she said, the students had a number of changes they wanted to see made to the syllabus. Wyatt pointed out that the Cayman Islands class he had meant to sign up for allowed for presentations around a firepit instead of essays; the identical twins (Fitger had no hope of ever telling them apart—both wore PAYNE: WHERE EDUCATION HURTS T-shirts) recommended replacing two or three of the assignments with a group project. As studio art majors aware that traditional materials might be scarce, they suggested collage.

Brent approved of the idea of a group project and wanted to know if Fitger had a tweezers. He had a splinter or an ingrown hair on his neck; it was driving him nuts.

Fitger did not have a tweezers—at least, not with him. He unfastened his seat belt and stood, noting that the floor by his stocking feet was strewn with detritus from the family in front of him: a sprinkling of raisins, several pieces of Lego, and the wakeful, one-eyed, ominous head of a doll. Toeing the doll's head out of the way, he told Lin and the other students that he would be happy to discuss the details of the syllabus when they were in England; for now, he would simply attempt to assuage their concerns by letting them know that the daily writing assignments were very short—only five hundred words—and the final essay would be based on their individual experiences and observations. The course requirements were in no way onerous and were safely within the guidelines for an "experience" class. As a teacher of writing, he would occasionally ask the students to revise, but he would be available for regular consults and feedback, which—

"Sir? Excuse me." A flight attendant in a *Star Trek*–inspired uniform interrupted. The aisle of the plane was not a meeting space, she said; and as was previously announced over the intercom, the rolling carts required an unobstructed path. He was impeding with the beverage service.

Fitger noted the unfortunate isosceles triangle of her uniform's neckline. " 'Impede,' " he said, "is a transitive verb. There's no need to use the word 'with.' "

The students—all but Felicity in the seat beside him—quickly dispersed. An hour later, when the plane began to shudder over Hudson Bay, he felt her reach for his hand.

Despite a few minor mishaps (one passport temporarily lost in an airport restroom, and one student—Wyatt—spilling a pint of beer onto a stranger's lap on the Underground), they traveled from Heathrow to Paddington to their dorm. The home away from home where they would live for the next three weeks was located in a suburb on the outskirts of London—a somewhat industrial area called Barking. They were greeted in the lobby by Herman Trout, a short, troll-like man who served as residential director, security, handyman, program manager, and (Fitger would soon learn) in-house narcoleptic: he kept a foldaway cot at reception, under the desk. Mr. Trout ("like the fish!" he grinned, his gnarled hand shaking Fitger's) distributed room keys and rattled through an orientation: Dinner wasn't served in the dorm on Sundays, but they would find vending machines in the alcove. Breakfast daily from eight to nine. Towels and sheets were on their beds. Smoking wasn't allowed. Their rooms—pardon the toolbox on the steps; he was fixing the handrail—were upstairs.

Fitger had been hoping that his faculty apartment might be distant from the students', perhaps in a far-flung sound-proof wing; but it was only a few steps away, at the end of the second-floor hall. It consisted of a windowless bedroom, a bathroom with a shower so small it resembled an upright plexiglass tube, and a living room/kitchen with a floral couch, a wooden table and chair which would serve as his workplace, and a mini-refrigerator and two-burner stove. The rooms were chilly in the way that only English rooms could be. Well, so be it. He hung his shirts on a row of clattering hangers, then investigated the kitchen cabinets, hoping for a basket of fruit or a beer, but found only a value pack of ant traps, a trio of coffee mugs, and a stiff yellow sponge. Music and laughter from the students' rooms filtered toward him. He sent Janet a text—*The eagle has landed*—without expecting or receiving a reply.

Fitger hadn't slept on the plane—the students had sought him out during the flight with a series of random questions—and, unsurprisingly, he was tired. He lay down for a quick nap (the mattress sagged in the middle and the pillows were as slim as lozenges) and began to sketch out his plan of attack for the following day. Janet underestimated him, he thought. When was the last time she'd seen him in the classroom? He closed his eyes. Day #1 of his allotted twenty-two days would involve an hour-long orientation followed by a group discussion, and an afternoon trip to the British Museum. He and Janet had spent a day there together. He remembered her standing mesmerized in front of an ancient chess set carved from whales' teeth. Was that correct? Whales' teeth? Or would they have been whales' bones? He imagined Janet scolding him for not being able to remember. He pictured her with a bottle of wine in her hand. They weren't in the museum anymore, they were at a restaurant, by the ocean, their table thickly spread with seaweed and shells. The restaurant was called Barking and their waiter was Rogaine. He handed them menus on which every dish was whale: fried fluke, filet of flipper . . . Janet ordered a blowhole. Fitger woke, fully dressed and wondering where he was, at 3:30 a.m.

He knew that an attempt to go back to sleep when he was no longer tired would only lead to rumination, incidents from his recent or far-flung past rising up through the murk of his mind like bitter bubbles released from a swamp. During insomniac moments he tended to remember, for example, his third-grade teacher, Mrs. Smalley, forcing him to write *I behaved badly in class today* on the chalkboard one hundred times. While others in his cohort had presumably been mastering long division, he had been forced to dedicate himself to that pointless task. Why would his mind's catalog keep something like that in circulation? Would these dreary snippets be the keepsakes of his senior years?

He heard a door open and close in the hallway but, getting up and looking through the peephole, he saw nothing. He decided to shower (arms at his sides to avoid all contact with the mildewed walls) and catch up on email he'd neglected in preparation for the trip. Where were the adapters he'd packed for the British outlets? He distinctly remembered zipping three of them (an extra adapter in case the first didn't work, and a third to lend to any absentminded student who had forgotten their own) into the side-zipper pocket of his suitcase. Hauling his large red suitcase out of the closet, he remembered that the side-zipper pocket was, in fact, in the smaller blue valise he had decided at the last minute not to bring with him. A thorough search of the apartment revealed no adapter. Perhaps he would find one in the lobby downstairs.

"Well. Took a tumble." This was Herman Trout, dressed in nightshirt and sweatpants, who had undoubtedly heard the sound of Fitger plunging headlong, in stocking feet, down the polished steps on his way to the lobby. The Trout switched on the light.

"I tripped on something." Stifling a howl, Fitger clutched at his leg. "There was something on the steps. A screwdriver. And a pile of screws."

No, nothing on the steps, the Trout said. And he didn't recommend pussyfooting about in the dark after hours. Did Fitger need to visit a clinic?

Fitger pulled up his pant leg to reveal the hairless knurl of a kneecap. His shinbone was dented and would surely bruise, and his ankle—he could feel it swelling—was probably sprained, but he could wiggle his toes. "It was a screwdriver," he insisted. "With a yellow handle. It must have been from your toolbox."

"Couldn't be. Put that box away hours ago." The Trout, perhaps adept at gaslighting the dorm's inhabitants, denied the possibility of any tools on the stairs.

Never mind, Fitger said. He pulled himself up. Did Herman have a spare adapter?

A man of few words—most of his sentences lacked pronouns—the Trout led the way down the hall, past the classroom and the cafeteria, Fitger limping along in his wake. They entered a storeroom full of buckets, brooms, ladders, and items travelers must have forgotten or abandoned: clothing, hair dryers, notebooks, headphones, and—dangling from a hook near the ceiling—a prosthetic arm. The Trout muttered to himself while combing through a bin of cords and electronics, Fitger noticing a collection of screwdrivers—most of them with yellow handles—in an open toolbox on the floor.

The Trout found an adapter. And he offered Fitger a walking stick. It was carved and painted to look like a snake, its head featuring a pair of red beaded eyes.

"You want me to use that?" Fitger asked.

The Trout shrugged and said it was up to Fitger, but the elevator was out of service, so he might find it useful, going up and down stairs.

A few hours later, his foot in a bucket of ice in the lobby, Fitger was waiting for the undergrads to get out of bed for their first day of class. Breakfast, the Trout reminded him, was over at nine; and during their first week in London, they would be sharing the cafeteria, the laundry room, and the dorm's only classroom with a group of European students, whose rooms were below them on the first floor. Fitger hadn't seen or heard these other students, but a stack of dirty dishes in a plastic tub indicated that they'd already eaten, and the door to the only classroom was closed. At 8:55, the Americans began to stagger downstairs.

One of the twins sidled up to the metal steam tray: sausage, muffins, a rack of toast, eggs bubbling in oil, and sliced tomatoes.

"Gross," she said. "What did you do to your leg?"

"It's just a sprain. Nothing serious."

Wyatt asked if Fitger had torn a ligament. Some sprains were serious—even worse than a broken bone. Did Fitger want him to examine the injury? He had taken a Wilderness First Responder course, and he knew first aid.

"Thank you, but no," Fitger said. He took his foot out of the bucket and pulled on a sock.

Lin wanted to know if his snake-head cane was from *The Lord of the Rings*.

The sole classroom being occupied when the students were settled, Fitger began their first session standing in front of the steam tray, leaning on his serpent's staff and reviewing the course requirements. The students would complete a five-hundred-word response to a prompt every day, after completing the activity or visiting the site specified on the syllabus. A single, more traditional five-to-seven-page essay would be due at the end of the term.

Brent raised his hand.

"Yes! A question?"

Brent wanted to know if anyone else wanted to eat the last sausage. And: Was there ketchup?

Joe Ballo (the other students, for reasons Fitger didn't understand, always referred to him by his first and last name) suggested that Brent use a tomato instead.

Fitger leaned back and put the palm of his hand in a puddle of egg yolk. As for their first day and their first assignment in London, he said, the students' task would be to travel via Underground to the British Museum, where they would each seek out an object of interest. They would describe said object in grammatical prose, making use of vivid and original detail.

All work should be titled, with a beginning, middle, and ending. The responses would be due before dinner, feedback to follow. In view of his injury—which was very minor, nothing for anyone to worry about—he would see them back at the dorm that afternoon.

Another student was raising her hand. Though searching his mind's deepest recesses, Fitger failed to come up with her name. What the hell was it? She was the one with the travel iron, and she was wearing a blouse, Fitger noticed, that looked particularly crisp. "I'm sorry," he said, "you'll have to remind me . . ."

"Sonia."

"Yes. Sonia. Of course." *S for Suitcases* = *Sonia.* "Apologies. You have a question?"

"Yeah. If you can't go, can that Rumpelstiltskin guy go with us?"

Herman Trout being asleep on a cot under the welcome desk, Fitger explained that the resident supervisor's job required that he remain at the dorm. "You'll be fine," he said. "You'll go as a group; you'll keep an eye out for each other and stick together. You've got your IDs and your travel cards, all eleven of you. It'll be an adventure." A student dressed entirely in black with the exception of a crimson scarf around his neck (the irritated splotch of skin above the scarf revealed this to be *E for Eczema* = *Elwyn*) announced that they weren't eleven. One student was missing.

"Missing?" Fitger did a quick head count. "Who isn't here?"

"D.B.," said one of the twins. Was this Andromeda or Cassiopeia? They were dressed alike again, in identical NO PLEA-

SURE WITHOUT PAYNE T-shirts. D.B. was probably sleeping in, she said. He had the room next to hers, and she had heard him come back to the dorm "at, like, three a.m."

Recalling the sound of a door clicking shut in the middle of the night, Fitger tried to conjure up D.B.'s image, but his memory offered only a dark knitted cap and the general impression of a slender individual who had barely spoken while on the plane. *D.B.* = *Decibel,* he thought.

Lin asked if the muffins were made with butter or egg and reminded Fitger that she was a vegan.

After telling her that he would investigate the muffins, he distributed an essay for group discussion. Not wanting to climb the stairs, he would let D.B. sleep, for the present. Remembering Janet's description of himself as a poorly social-ized person, he decided that affability would be the best way to start off the term.

At noon, the undergrads—including D.B., who wore his knit-ted hat and sunglasses even indoors—left en masse for the British Museum. Fitger retired to his quarters with a bag of ice for his ankle and logged on to email. He had come to under-stand that the job of department chair consisted primarily of attempting to dispose of email, his daily task the triage and forwarding and deletion of an ever-replenishing queue of demands, entreaties, chastisements, threats, and precautions, which usually included a dozen communiqués in ALL CAPS from the English Department administrator, Fran, who des-ignated even the most trivial messages with the subject line

URGENT. She was reminding him that another installment of near-meaningless online forms had to be filed within the next few days.

Well, he would attend to the forms soon enough, because here was an email from JSMatthias@Payne.edu. Was Janet wishing him luck on his first full day in England? No: she was letting him know that she had rescheduled the dog's checkup. She sent the new date and time and noted that a sedative (for the dog) might be in order; Fitger knew how much Rogaine hated the vet. Fitger sent her an email in return, omitting any reference to the taser at the airport or his swollen ankle but telling her about his dream of Rogaine being their waiter. *He was very dapper in his restaurant whites,* he wrote. By the way, how was the job search going? Had Janet polished her résumé? Fitger would be happy to look it over, if that might be useful. He looked at his watch. It was early morning at Payne; she was probably drinking her first cup of coffee.

His cell phone, recently charged, began to buzz. Fitger resented the recent trend toward multiple, excess forms of communication—the need to make oneself available via email and cell and landline, text, tweet, Post-It note, and carrier pigeon. But he had been told that, while in England, he was "on duty" 24/7. He put on his glasses and peered at the screen. One of the students was informing him that the group, after getting lost at King's Cross for a while, had reached the museum. It was pretty cool, actually. Huge! And: There were mummies—a big collection of them. From Egypt. Would it be okay to write about the mummies?

Yes, Fitger answered.

A follow-up text: *What if more than one student wants to write about the mummies?*

One letter of the alphabet at a time (he texted slowly), Fitger responded: Surely there was more than one thing a person could notice and describe about a collection of ancient dead bodies.

Haha yeah.

He returned to email on his computer. Janet had replied to his message. She didn't need any help with her résumé; she was perfectly capable of explaining what she did for a living. What were he and his students up to?

Fitger responded: *First assignment. I sent them to the British Museum. Are you going to need references?*

His phone lit up with a new series of texts from the undergrads. The instructions he had provided said they had to use details in their writing: Did those have to be details a person could see? Or could they write about things like the Egyptians pulling a dead person's brain out through their nose? And: If more than one person wanted to write about the mummies, why couldn't they do a group project?

No group projects, Fitger answered, pecking out his response. Going back to his laptop, he found he'd been booted from the wifi. Where was the password? He had carefully written it down somewhere. He logged in again and found a new email from Janet. What did he mean he *sent* his students to the British Museum? Wasn't he with them?

No, he trusted them to go on their own, he said. They were fine. But what about references? Would Janet need someone to write her a letter?

A new sequence of texts from the undergrads informed Fitger that Xanna didn't feel well. She was throwing up in the women's restroom. A subgroup of students was going to bring her back in a cab.

"Shit." He tried to remember which of the undergrads Xanna was. Perhaps the student with the worried parent? He envisioned a coffin in the overhead compartment on the return trip to Payne and tried to send a text to an *X. Blythe* but was rebuffed with "Failure to Send."

He emailed Janet. *If you need a recommendation you should let me know.*

Ha, she wrote. *Don't be absurd.*

Someone—Fitger didn't know who it was; the students' texts were attached to phone numbers rather than names— sent him a photo of a crystal skull. No message. Hmm. Fitger replied with a question mark, then returned to his correspondence with Janet. *I won't mention that we used to be married.* He reminded her that he had a particular flair when it came to the writing of recommendations.

That particular flair is not one that I want to rely on, Janet wrote. She told him she would sooner ask Frank. ***And this is still confidential.***

Who's Frank? Fitger asked. The bag of ice on his leg was melting; limping, he carried it into the bathroom and dropped it in the sink.

His phone was buzzing; it nearly fell off the desk. *We are looking for taxis now,* said a group message from the students. Would the professor pay for their cab fare to bring Xanna back? She was still throwing up.

Yes, he wrote, while wondering if it was too early to start

40

counting the number of days until the end of the trip. Perhaps he could notch them into the wall beside his desk.

Janet responded: Frank was the guy from Buildings and Grounds who, every spring, was responsible for the enormous floral "P.U." arrangement, in school colors, on the president's lawn. *He's got a Martin Van Buren haircut.*

While Fitger was googling Martin Van Buren, the students texted to ask if he would pay for two cabs. Or maybe three. Because most of them were tired of the museum. They had already been there for almost an hour.

Fitger texted them back. They were finished with two million years of human history in fifty-five minutes? Then he emailed Janet again. *Let me know if Frank is unavailable. My offer stands. Are you off to work soon?*

She didn't answer. This was what Fitger hated about e-conversation: no one ever said goodbye; they just vanished, as if disappearing into a mist.

The students sent a new text: *Never mind about the second cab. We found some other places we want to go.*

What kind of places? Fitger asked.

But neither this, nor his question to Janet, received a reply.

FOUR

A & C (ANDROMEDA AND CASSIOPEIA)
WAGNER-HALL

BRITISH MUSEUM OBJECT DESCRIPTION

Note: This is a two-part project; the other half is in your cubby mailbox on the first floor.

The British Museum's Cyrus Cylinder is a corncob-shaped object made of clay, from Babylonia 6th century BC. It is close to the size and color of an old corncob, yellowish-brown with a crack down the middle and a bite taken out of the crack. 45 lines of writing, Akkadian cuneiform, circle the cob. The writing talks about a king named Cyrus who called himself Cyrus the Great and sometimes King of the Universe. He liked to talk about the wars he won and the other kings who kissed his feet, and other examples of His Greatness, like his personal relationship with Marduk, a Mesopotamian god. Basically we're talking about a masculinist brag sheet on an ear of corn.

The visual art half of our project (we put it in your cubby) is a prototype we're calling the Cynthia Cylinder. We made it from two interlocking toilet-paper tubes with part of a brown paper bag wrapped around. (We would have rather submit-ted an actual corncob with writing on it, but couldn't find any corn.

Some Questions Our Project Brings Up:
1) How does the shape or material of an artwork affect the viewer's experience?
2) Why do viewers (most of the kids on this trip) want art to be representative, or they want it explained?

The writing on the Cynthia Cylinder is our own version of cuneiform—we haven't fig-ured this part out yet, but it should be a script only women can read. A translation of the cuneiform will explain that the cob is printed with a list of reasons why women are genetically superior to men, starting with the extra X-chromosome and long-term survival advantages, and ending with their ability to see more colors than men.

We emailed Profes-sor Wayetu about this project and she is enthusiastic. She suggested a performance-oriented ver-sion with the text being projected onto a corncob (real or handmade) and changing depending on the gender of the viewer. We will consider this possibility when we get back to Payne.

JOE BALLO FIRST ASSIGNMENT
DESCRIPTION OF AN OBJECT

The place I observed and will describe for this assignment is the Foundling Museum. This is a place I went on my own after one of the students in our group got sick. I didn't think anyone else would want to see it, we all went our own ways.

The Foundling Museum is not far from the British Museum. I looked it up on my phone and walked. It is a distance of about ten blocks.

Foundling is an old word that people don't say much anymore. It means a baby or kid whose parents have to give him away. In England starting in the 1700s this happens a lot.

The museum is small. It has films and information and it tells about foundlings and their lives and sometimes the parents who gave them up. Here is a question worth asking: Is it worse for the parents or the kids?

If we are supposed to describe an object the one I will choose is a token. A token in the Foundling Museum is something a mother left behind when she gave up her kid. Sometimes it was a coin with scratches on it. Sometimes a piece of fabric ripped in half maybe from an apron or the woman's dress. She gave half to the Foundling Museum and kept half for herself. So someday maybe she could come back and show her half of the token and say that kid is mine here is my proof and she could have him again.

Most of the time that didn't happen. The mothers left their tokens and wrote letters and said please give this letter to my son but they never did. And the son never knew about the token or saw his mother again.

I looked at the tokens for a long time. Especially the one that looked like a dog tag, silver and flat with a hole for a chain. The words on it in cursive said this is a token. Like the mother couldn't think of what to write but she was putting a marker down to say that is my son. I thought about her making that token maybe scratching the words onto it with a nail or a pin it must have taken some time. Her son most likely never saw it and never knew she was thinking about him and never saw her again.

The Foundling Museum is not a hospital or an orphanage anymore which it used to be. It is a museum. There are not many orphanages in the US these days it is mostly people being moved into foster homes. I was in two different foster homes so I had that experience. I am not complaining others have had it worse but I do have nightmares sometimes to this day.

I took a picture of the token and was going to include it here but decided not to because you told us to describe, which I have done what I can. I deleted the picture from my phone because I didn't want it. Now I am up to 500 words.

SONIA MORALES

ASSIGNMENT #1 PROFESSOR FIGURE

I will start by saying that Brent and I didn't find anything to write about in the British Museum which is really crowded with all kinds of different stuff, so we decided to fulfill a lifelong dream of mine and go to the wax museum at Madam Tussaud's. I was supposed to go a few years ago with my cousin to the Las Vegas Madam Tussaud but she had her appendix out (at first I thought she was faking, believe me Tina has pulled that kind of s*** before) so we couldn't go.

You might be surprised that Brent and I went together but no one else in our group was interested which I thought was a shame. I thought one of the other girls at least would go along but to be honest I am not hitting it off with them very well because some of them think they are better than everyone else (and personally I think that twins who still dress the same when they are in college are immature). Anyway, Brent said he wanted to see the sports wax figures and I wanted to see the wax J.Lo and Selena. Brent said he would buy us tickets online. We went as friends.

When we got there people were waiting to get in, even the people like us who had tickets. The guy in line in front of us had a huge streak of bird-doo on his back, we thought of letting him know but in the end we didn't say anything.

Inside the museum Brent was disappointed about there not being very many basketball players but he was a good sport. We started to have a good time and we were talking about other times when we used to hang out. (We have known each other since the seventh grade.) I was thinking, here is the Brent I remembered from last year, the one who would text me a picture of a cup of coffee in the morning and when I opened my door a skim latte (which is what I drink every morning and I have not found one here so far 😔) would be waiting for me.

To be honest I was maybe wishing we didn't break up because everyone makes mistakes and Brent definitely made his but most of the time I have known him he has been a nice guy.

We took pictures of each other for our Insta, he took a picture of me with Tyra Banks. She is really tall and in wax she looks good. It was maybe halfway through the museum I almost bumped into a lady who didn't speak English (I said Sorry but she was still rude) and a minute later Brent was holding my hand. I don't know how it started but there it was. Things you don't predict sometimes can happen that way.

I got emotional all the sudden, I mean we were far away from home and even our professor wasn't with us so other than Brent I was alone.

Brent saw that I was choked up, we were at the King Kong area, he put his arm around me and I saw him take something out of his pocket. It was his grandmother's ring that I already knew about, he had showed it to me before. He loved his grandma a lot. (She is dead.)

I wasn't sure I should put it on. To be honest it is not a ring I would of picked out myself, my birthstone is topaz (yellow) and this ring is a garnet with a dent on one side and it looked like a piece of hair or something was caught in the part that holds the stone.

Brent said it wasn't a going steady or engagement ring or even close, he was planning to give it to me for my birthday before we broke up and now it was a ring to say he still cares about me and he was thinking about us and he felt bad. And I could wear the ring or not, it was up to me.

The King Kong's eyes blinked back and forth. I took a picture of the ring for my mom, she has always liked Brent a lot, I used to joke her around by saying she loved my boyfriend better than me.

I am not sure if I am going to wear it because we are technically (for now) broken up.

We knew this assignment was due at 5 (I had to shower I will have mine in by 9) so we finished the museum and went back to the dorm.

ELWYN YANG

PROFESSOR FITGER PAPER #1

THE MYSTERY OF THE CRYSTAL SKULL

Come in, come in, and don't be afraid! Welcome to the Wellcome Trust Gallery, Room 24 in the British Museum. I am the crystal skull you see before you in the glass enclosure at the center of the room.

You may have heard about me as I am a legend—but you may not touch me! I am hewn of rock crystal, a substance known for its enigmatical capabilities. The Aztecs of Brazil made use of me in their bloody rituals. The things I have witnessed over the centuries with my crystal eyes can scarce be described.

Come closer! Other visitors neglect me—only YOU can hear my voice and feel the power of my influence.

NOW HEED AND ATTEND ME, FOR I HAVE BEEN WAITING, AND THERE ARE MANY IMPORTANT THINGS THAT I NEED TO EXPLAIN. What's that? You wonder why no one else listens when I speak? Don't concern yourself with the others: they are shallow fools . . . See how the light shines in the silver wells of my empty eye sockets? That's better! There! You are listening now, you are relaxed . . .

I can trust you now with my sacred knowledge. You know that I was once owned by Tiffany's, a famous jewelry store in New York, and before that I lived with an antiques dealer in Paris. But my keepers didn't know what I yearned for! I have waited centuries . . .

What? You say that your classmates are leaving the museum?

Without waiting for you even though you were supposed to stay together? Let them go! They are pitter-patter mortals, unworthy of my sacred knowledge. YOUR PLACE IS IN ROOM 24. YOU WILL STAY HERE WITH ME AND ABIDE MY COMMANDS . . .

You understand that I am one of the thirteen crystal skulls? And that when the thirteen are brought together we will unleash our omnipotent power and prophesy the future? Good, good!

Do you see the guard over there? The one with the key to my glass case dangling from his belt?

YOU WILL NOT ARGUE WITH ME! YOU ARE THE ONE I HAVE CHOSEN, THE ONLY ONE STRONG ENOUGH TO OBEY!

You have found the obsidian knife in your pocket . . . I see your trembling fingers testing its blade . . .

YOU MUST LISTEN TO ME! THE OTHERS HAVE LEFT AND YOU ARE ALONE. THERE IS NO ESCAPE FROM THE THUNDEROUS DOMINION OF MY VOICE!

Are you walking softly now toward the guard? IT WILL BE SO EASY TO SLIP THE KNIFE ACROSS HIS THROAT AND TAKE THE KEYS! KEEP GOING. YES! A FEW MORE STEPS, A FEW MORE STEPS, AND YOU WILL FREE ME TO FULFILL MY DESTINY . . .

Felicity Babinec

Describing an Object in the British Museum

The old disagreement about whether dogs or cats are better was put to rest a few thousand years ago by the Egyptians who decided the matter once in for-all. They answered this question by making cats one of their major goddesses. Her name was Bastet. She was worshipped and idolized with the Egyptians often getting buried with their cats.

I wish our group had stayed together in the British Museum but after the mummy exhibit some people went off on their own. I didn't want to be by myself so I followed Cassie and Andromeda for a while (I don't think they minded that I was following) and we walked past a statue of the Gayer-Anderson cat. This is a bronze Egyptian statue from a temple. It is sculpted with a bunch of necklaces (that part of it is bronze, it is hard to describe), and the statue wears gold earrings and a matching nose ring which I hope no Egyptian ever tried to put on their pet. The reason it is the Gayer-Anderson cat is that is the name of the man who gave the statue to the museum. It was made around 600 BC.

Cats are definitely a better choice if you are going to turn an animal into a god. Number one, they are cleaner, and if a cat is going to be in a temple (like the Gayer-Anderson cat I think was), you would want it to be very clean. Number two, cats have more dignity than dogs and are more polite. No one would want a god who is jumping up at the dinner table or rolling in mud on the ground. Number three, they are quieter and softer and have excellent night vision. Most cats I have known are very smart.

I don't have a lot more to describe about the Gayer-Anderson cat, I didn't spend a lot of time looking at it because Cassie and Andromeda weren't very interested (they are art majors, I have never known an art major before!) and I didn't want to be alone so I went to other parts of the museum with them. But I can tell you that this sculpture of a cat is sort of green in color, a thin cat sitting up tall with its tail curled nicely around its side.

A lot of people have written about cats, including a poet named T.S. Eliot who made a Broadway show that is really famous. I have the CD. My favorite song is The Rum Tum Tugger.

I will end by saying
That if I were an Egyptian I would definitely be praying
To a cat in my temple
Because it is simple—
Cats are the best pets on earth
And no other creature has a cats' worth.

P.S. I hope this is not too long. If it is you can take off the poem at the end.

P.S.S. I am excited to be here in England (but still kind of nervous, it is my first time).

WYATT FRANKLIN,
PROFESSOR FITGER, HOMEWORK #1

Our first day in England I was tired AF since a group of us stayed up most of the night before in my room. Sometimes you party and feel fine, sometimes you wake up and feel like the slime at the bottom of a bucket. That's how it is with me anyway, and it is worse in the winter. Also I forgot to repack my duffel from when I thought we were going to the Cayman Islands so I had to wear my cargo shorts and damn it was cold.

We didn't know what to look at when we got to the British Museum until somebody mentioned Egyptian mummies, so that's where we went. This is an exhibit you definitely wish you had drugs for, because there are bodies lying on shelves and gold coffins standing up behind glass, and the bodies are wrapped in some kind of Egyptian ace bandages. There are coffins for animals. One girl on our trip freaked out when she saw the mummy of a cat. The Egyptians took some of the body parts out and stored them in jars, the way your grandmother would probably make jam.

The part I decided to write about is the Egyptian Book of the Dead. It's like a pamphlet or scroll the dead Egyptian would put in his coffin and it had pictures and written instructions telling the dead guy how to get to the other side through the land of the dead. The book was kind of like a form you need to have when you go through customs, except that instead of the British customs guys in their little booths you are showing your *I am dead* paperwork to demons and serpents and to a bunch of pissed-off dog-headed gods who might hang you upside down and make you eat your own turds. (I am not making that up.) At the end if the gods let you through, one of the dog-headed guys weighs your heart on a scale. That part is like avoiding the booby traps and coming to the end of the greatest pinball game you will ever play.

The real name for the Book of the Dead is the Book of Coming Forth By Day, but that probably sounded too much like an AA or an NA meeting (I have been in both and should probably start up again) and I guess The Book of the Dead had a better sound. The thing I liked about it is: everybody wants a map of how not to let life (or death if you are Egyptian) fuck them over, you want to avoid the sandtraps and get to the end. One of my best friends in high school got killed in a car accident (his name was Lowell, we used to hang out all the time) and I thought about Low having a set of directions telling him not to get in the car that night (our friend Jack was driving, the roads were icy, I wasn't there) or maybe directions for after he was dead, about avoiding the dog-head gods who would make him eat his own shit. (Low had a good sense of humor, I used to stop by his parents now and then but whenever I see his dad now he cries.)

I took some pictures of the Book of the Dead to look at later because someone in our group was getting sick, you could hear it from outside the bathroom a sound like things coming up from a drain. Anyway, I like the idea of having instructions for life/death written down to bring with you. It would be like someone helping you pack for a trip except you get into your suitcase and it is also a coffin. I obviously suck at packing and would be better off with a different set of instructions than the ones I have been following in the last few years but that is a story for another time.

VOMITING IN THE BRITISH MUSEUM: AN EXPERIENCE

You are in a stall in the women's bathroom in the British Museum with a spot of vomit on your shoe when your mom sends a text.

Hi honey! Doing OK so far? Everything good?

You are not finished vomiting because here is that pressing-up feeling under your jaw, your mouth refilling itself like a well full of spit. But you text her OK because she already texts you a lot and she will definitely up her game if she's worried. When it comes to worrying she is a specialist.

Your first day in London! she says.

Yup. You breathe in and out and stare into the hole in the center of the toilet. You vomit and flush.

What's on your schedule today? your mom asks.

You leave the stall and wash your hands at the sink and text her back to tell her you're in the British Museum. Like most museums this one will culminate in a gift shop. What should you bring her? A souvenir?

U know I don't need any gifts, she says. Just U safe & sound. She wants to know if the other kids on the trip are nice.

You send her a neutral/maybe face.

One step at a time, she says. That's the way to make friends! No over-thinking!

You send her an emoji of a tornado next to a brain.

She says hahaha and sends you a heart.

You send her a picture of a piece of broccoli, just to be random.

The bathroom door opens, and two of the girls from the trip are studying your white-washed face in the mirror. One of them says that maybe you are sleep deprived due to jet lag or maybe you ate one of those weird-looking eggs at breakfast. Or maybe you're pregnant?

Haha you're not pregnant.

The second girl tells you about the museum's Egyptian mummies which she says are like moldy sleeping beauties in coffins.

Nice metaphor, you tell her. You go back to the stall and throw up.

Your mom texts again. She tells you she is glad you're having an adventure in England but she hopes you'll remember what the campus therapist said about taking care of yourself, you shouldn't overextend. She tells you that sometimes you don't know when to stop.

You text her a picture of a stop sign. She texts you another heart, and then a unicorn with a bunch of balloons.

The two girls from your trip announce, through the door of your stall, that most of the group is getting ready to leave the museum. The lovey-dovey couple is planning to go to Madam Tussaud's. Do you want to go with them? No. You make a bet with yourself: one of them will be hooking up with someone else in your group before the trip is done.

You tell the girls you'll be out in a minute. You text your mom and tell her you're sorry for being such a problem child.

She texts back to tell you she loves you. And she sends you a picture of a bee and a knee. This is her shorthand: *You are the bees' knees.*

You take a deep breath and come out of the stall to find one of the guys from the trip, the one who is wearing shorts because he apparently thought England was in the Caribbean, leaning against the paper towel dispenser. His legs are furry with hair and he doesn't seem to care that he is a guy in a women's restroom. He offers you some chalky pink pills. He has a plastic bag full of pills in his cargo shorts pocket, back home he is probably a dealer, and you can tell by the slow way he's blinking that he's probably high. You take one of the flat pink disks and chew it slowly.

When you leave the bathroom, a wad of damp paper towels in hand, the girl who is obsessed with her cat says she's sorry you're sick. And she wants to know what you'll do about your first essay. How will you write it, if you weren't able to see the museum?

You tell her you're going to write about throwing up. And you'll call your essay "Vomiting in the British Museum." She probably thinks you aren't serious, but of course you are.

BRENT SCHRAFT, PROF. FITGER'S FIRST ASSIGNMENT #1

(this is not for a grade you said we could revise our first one)

For my first, assignment the thing I will describe is a wax museum, called Madame Tussaud. Me and Sonia went there but, we are going to describe different things. Anyway this is a museum of wax dummies Sonia always wanted to see it so, that is why we are there.

We did some poses for Sonia and my's Instagram, we have a joint account SoniaandBrent. We went to the wax athlete section I thought the museum would have a Jordan or Kobe or LeBron so I could do my hook shot against them I was famous for in my high school my senior, year. Our team The Red Tigers isn't that good anymore I think they went two-and-twelve last season and not because of Mr. DiGiddio he is the coach, their center sucks. But the Tussaid museum since it is England had cricket players not basketball, it is mostly a game for people of foreign dissent. I had a part scholarship and would still be playing at Payne but messed up my knee, an anterior ligament with surgery which in hind-side maybe I shouldn't done. I am 5-eleven, 175 not as trim as I could be but still solid on the muscular side. I keep in shape. Sonia jogs and watches her figure she always looks good, I took a picture of her with the queen. I know she wrote about the ring I gave her, she showed her me essay but I am writing my own, which was my grandmas (the ring) so I will mention that here. I admit I messed up in the passed but I am trying to make a mend, that is why I brought the ring on this trip. Sonia knows how much I cared about my grandma, she slept with me my whole freshman year after she died and I would tell her how sweet she was.

Anyway, the photo I put on our Instagram was me with Anthony Joshua, a boxer he is a heavyweight 6 foot 6 his arms are ripped, at the Olympics he got a gold. I have done some boxing but not very serious, it is hard to have a sport that is yours (basketball) and then, give it up. Anyway that is what me and Sonia saw and did at our museum. The way the statues take four or six months to make and cost 150 thousand pounds which is more than that in American dollars. Also that the real Madam Tussauds was an actual person (she was French) who used chopped off heads from a guillotine to learn about her job.

PS Let me know if I can do extra credit for this class I know my writing needs work but I am not taking it for granite, I will work hard.

LIN JEN SNOW

FIRST ESSAY

The British museum is a display of illegally trafficked items the British ripped off from other countries during their imperialist pillaging attacks around the world. Some of the things they have stolen and refuse to return include actual dead human remains, valuable historical relics and religious icons, and artwork they like to pretend that other countries are too poor or violent or stupid to take care of. A walk through any gallery in this warehouse of stolen goods should make most people want to set up a Kickstarter to get Queen Victoria's coffin displayed in Bhutan.

One of the largest stolen items (not counting the Parthenon which was ripped off by a British ambassador named Elgin and then SOLD to the museum, because why not make the most of exploitation) is the Easter Island statue, Hoa Hakananai'a. This was taken without permission from Rapa Nui* by the British Navy in 1868. The commodore of a ship forced the native people to dig it out of the ground and hand it over, an important piece of their own culture. The statue is a moai, incredibly meaningful to the people on Rapa Nui and their religion. They have asked for it back multiple times. The people who run this

---

* The original and correct name for the island is Rapa Nui; the Dutch showed up and named it Easter. Anyone who thinks the Dutch were a bunch of gentle people growing tulips in wooden shoes just needs to look to South Africa.

museum might as well build a jungle gym out of dead people's bones.

The instructions for this assignment are to describe an object in the museum but I believe doing that for Hoa Hakananai'a would make me complicit. I would say you should see the statue for yourself but that would be just as bad because people who want to see it should have to go to Rapa Nui. People who argue against returning the statue say it will deteriorate out in the open. The Taj Mahal is probably deteriorating, too but so far no one has suggested moving it to South Dakota so Americans can drive their SUVs and trucks to see it. (If they went to India they would probably complain about the spice in the food.)

I wasted ten minutes arguing about Hoa Hakananai'a and the Great Thieving Colonialist History of the entire museum with some of the other students on this trip who obviously need to take a history or a politics class, because most of them don't seem familiar with the basic facts or outcome of colonialist rule and don't want to face up to their own complicity. A latinx student—whose family members are immigrants—wouldn't even acknowledge the fact of US imperialism on the border with Mexico.

I am hoping the other places we visit will be less problematic. I wish I hadn't seen the Hoa Hakananai'a even if it is incredibly beautiful and amazing. It should not be in London. I have deleted the pictures of the statue from my phone.

D. B. MELNYK

ASSIGNMENT #1

FIVE

Fitger stayed behind again on the students' second day in England and missed their visit to Covent Garden and the Benjamin Franklin House (where Elwyn was delighted to learn about the discovery of human remains in the inventor's basement). But, having procured an Ace bandage, he announced at dinner after the students' return that he would be well enough to join them on Day #3, for their Westminster Abbey tour.

Across from him at the table, Wyatt sliced into a sausage, which emitted a jet of warm porcine oil. He had noticed that Fitger had given up the snake-headed cane. Was his ankle still swollen?

"It's fine," Fitger said. He wiped the oil from his sleeve.

Lin, who was seated beside him, and who seemed to be subsisting mainly on plastic packets of ramen, announced in a tone of indignation that her meal had been poisoned with slaughterhouse fats.

Swelling, Wyatt told Fitger, was entirely normal after a sprain, but he should have had the foot looked at. Did he want to go shopping?

"Shopping?" Fitger asked. "Shopping for what?"

63

"Shoes." Wyatt pointed down at their feet. He wore a pair of plastic sandals, and Fitger one business shoe and one L.L.Bean slipper. "You should size up if your foot is still swollen," he said. "You could get a high-top—something soft, you know, but with ankle support. You need good support after a sprain."

The other students had finished their meal and were getting up. Fitger's silverware was missing. He thought about using his hands to eat his sausage and boiled potato.

"Rest, ice, compression, and elevation," Wyatt said. "RICE. That's something I learned as a Wilderness First Responder. That's the course that I took. I signed up with a friend, but I went alone."

Was the friend the one who had died? Fitger wondered. He wanted to offer his condolences but wasn't sure how to raise the subject. He told Wyatt that he would go with him to the shoe store. Thirty minutes later, the Trout called them a cab.

One-on-one interactions with students outside the classroom, Fitger thought, were invariably awkward. At Payne, when he ran into undergrads at the pharmacy or the mini-grocery, he felt as if two different species, otter and zebra, were meeting face-to-face at a watering hole. On the way to the shoe store in the cab, noticing Wyatt's red-rimmed eyes (drugs? depression?), he skirted the subject of Wyatt's first-aid training and asked about his studies at Payne. Did Fitger remember correctly that he was majoring in something related to health?

"Yeah. It's called health sciences." Bobbing his head to some internal tune, Wyatt confessed that he had "partied too hard" during the previous year. "And then bio-chem with Professor Clary really bit me in the ass."

Fitger was acquainted with Monroe Clary—an elongated man with a habit of parking an index finger, horizontally, under his nose. Clary seemed to take particular pleasure in recounting the percentages, year by year, of students he had managed to weed from his classes. Fitger said something to Wyatt along the lines of one path closing and another revealing itself to be open. Presumably recognizing a hackneyed phrase when he heard it, Wyatt shrugged.

The cab threaded its way through the streets of Barking, narrowly missing several cars and pedestrians. While they stopped at a light, Fitger saw a woman on the sidewalk combing through a trash can and weeping. The light turned green and they left her behind.

"You know, it's not like I still thought we were going to the Caymans," Wyatt said. "I made that mistake when I filled out the wrong form, but later I knew we were going to England. I just didn't repack, so that was on me."

"A lot of people procrastinate," Fitger said.

"Maybe. But, hey, I fucked up. Because that's who I am. You can't do pre-med with a D in bio-chem."

Again, Fitger wanted to bring up the subject of Wyatt's deceased friend. He also wanted to say something cutting about Monroe Clary. "Wyatt, you know that pre-med isn't the only—"

"Yeah, that's what everybody says. The possibilities. And I get it. But I *think* about stuff all the time and I can't keep my head straight, that's the thing." Wyatt toyed with the cab's ashtray, posted with a NO SMOKING sticker. "Like, I'll be in class, telling myself to pay attention, to take notes and stuff, but then class will be over and I've just sat there. Do you ever feel pissed because you know you could be a better person, you could be different, but you feel stuck just being yourself?"

Fitger felt he had just listened to his own very condensed autobiography. "Wyatt, I hope you're able to see that—"

The cab came to a halt. "Fifteen pounds even," the driver shouted through the plastic window between back seat and front. "Cash if you've got it."

"Do you want me to pay?" Wyatt asked.

"No." Fitger riffled through his wallet and came up with the bills. They got out of the cab.

"You can lean on me if you want to," Wyatt said. He extended his arm.

Fitger thanked him but said he would be fine.

JOSEPH BALLO

ASSIGNMENT #3, WRITE A LETTER
(TO SEND OR NOT) TO A PERSON AT HOME

Dear Uncle Royce, I am your nephew Joseph and I am writing this letter as part of my assignment for class. It is not a letter I will send. I have sent you letters to you and Aunt Syl and didn't hear back. The last one was returned to me unopen in a bigger envelope with my address and Joseph Nathan Ballo my full name. So I expect you are keeping track and you know where I am.

You maybe never expected though that now I am in England. Some of the things that I have seen here are: three different museums and the Trafalgar Square. You maybe never thought when I was fourteen and being sent away that I would get this far. I did not expect it as well. When we last saw each other and I told you I was sorry for all the harm, you turned away. You would not look at me. When I wrote you didn't write back. I believe that a person who does a thing by accident but not bad intention—

"You probably hate reading this stuff, don't you," Xanna said. "All the writing you make us turn in." It was late afternoon on Day #4, and the group was back from the Tate Museum, which Brent had apparently found disappointing. Fitger was reading the essays from the previous day's excursion in the lobby downstairs.

67

"I mean, nothing we write is going to be new or interesting." Xanna stood with her back to him by the beverage cart: tea was available every weekday afternoon. "And most of our essays probably suck."

Fitger watched her stack and unstack a number of cups before selecting one. "Actually, you write very well," he said. "Though I notice that you generally ignore the instructions."

Xanna unwrapped a tea bag and dropped it into her cup. "Yeah, that's one of the reasons I don't do very well in most of my classes. I like to do my own thing. I have an idea for something I want to write about the London Eye."

Fitger nodded absently while perusing Xanna's Westminster Abbey essay, which made almost no reference to the Gothic church. But it did include a categorization of her fellow students.

Introverts	III
Extroverts	IIII
Marxists	I
Presbyterians	I
Libertarians	I
Sophomores	III
Art hounds	II
Bad-asses	I
Elf	I

He wondered who the elf was. Of course, her scant description of the abbey wasn't surprising: Xanna had felt unwell twenty minutes into their tour and returned to the dorm. Fitger was waiting for her intestinal disturbance, which had first manifested itself in a women's restroom in the British Museum, to scourge the group like a biblical plague, but so far, no one else had been sick. "Are you feeling better today?" he asked.

She stirred four or five packets of sugar into her tea. "I'd give myself a seven out of ten. Now and then I still feel shitty. It comes and goes."

Fitger responded with a sympathetic hum. There was something familiar about her, he thought—something about the leftward tilt of her head when she spoke. $X = Xanna;$ she still lacked a mnemonic. Her blunt-cut hair was the verdigris color of a piece of copper left in the rain. "You know you're free to revise," he said. "You've been sick, so if you want to take the rest of the afternoon to—"

"Sorry. Hang on," Xanna said. "I have to answer a text from my mom. She worries if I take more than five seconds to text her back."

Fitger watched as her fingers twitched across the phone's small screen. Her nails were ragged, bitten down to the quick. Again he was sure he knew her from somewhere: maybe she worked at the campus library or in one of the offices at Payne. He turned back to his pile of essays.

"Ha. She told me to say hi for her to my prof," Xanna said. "And she hopes you won't fail me."

"Why would I fail you?"

"Oh, you know. I make people impatient. Do you actually care if our essays are any good?"

"Why are you asking me that?" He looked up.

"Well, I know it's your job and all that." She paused to sip from her cup of tea. "But do you think anyone's going to give a shit about my impressions of Buckingham Palace?"

"No," he said. She was right; she made him impatient. "*I* don't care about your impressions of Buckingham Palace. But I want you to know what they are, and I want you to be able to express them."

A corner of Xanna's lip curled up in a smile. Fitger castigated himself: he should have responded with a motivational speech, previewing the marvels that awaited her during the rest of her time in England. Oxford! Stonehenge! Though personally he was counting the days until the return to Heathrow, he had been charged with instilling in his students a sense of wonder in regard to the Soggy Isle, a desire to capture in their essays vivid impressions that would glow, in years to come, like polished stones in their minds. He told Xanna that he hoped she would feel well enough for their visit to Hampton Court the next day.

"Yeah, I probably will," she said. "But it's not a big deal if I have to miss it. D.B. obviously won't be there."

Why did she say that? Fitger asked. Was D.B. sick?

"No. He left."

"What do you mean, 'left'?" Again, he felt himself getting annoyed.

"I mean, he's not here," Xanna said, as if explaining something to a small child. "He's not in England. He took the Chunnel to Paris last night."

Fitger stared. "He can't go to Paris."

"I guess you should tell him that," Xanna said, while setting her empty cup on the tray, "maybe when he gets back."

Janet had been right, Fitger thought, *about the challenges inherent in teaching abroad.* Teaching of any sort reminded him of his fallibility, each course a fresh opportunity for self-doubt and regret. (Should he have required more—or less—work of his students? Lectured more often, or tried to keep his mouth shut?) But the English Experience presented an original set of pedagogical problems. During the previous forty-eight hours, he had spoken to the twins about their request for a nude model (Fitger quashed this idea, though Wyatt was willing); he had learned that cats with any length (or absence) of tail could win at least second place in a cat show; and he had emailed and texted and called D.B., threatening to confiscate his passport. In return, D.B. had sent him a photo of the Eiffel Tower and a short, breezy message, saying he'd be back in the U.K. soon.

It was only Day #6 and Fitger was fast approaching instructional fatigue. There was no hour of the day during which he was free of his students. He'd been woken in the middle of the night—twice when someone had misplaced the key to their room, and once when Joe Ballo, the sleepwalking claustrophobe, had gotten stuck in a bathroom stall. When the malfunctioning lock on the door was removed (the Trout employing a familiar-looking yellow screwdriver), Joe had emerged, quaking and drenched in sweat, a runnel of blood trickling out of his nose.

"You know what the problem with this class is?" Brent asked. They were seated in cuplike plastic chairs at a three-legged table in the second-floor hall, a makeshift conference area between the men's room and the stairs.

"No," Fitger said. "Why don't you tell me what the problem is."

"Okay. The problem," Brent said, one hand deep in a bag of potato chips, "is that you keep giving us too much work. Like, I shouldn't have to rewrite a paper I already did."

Fitger stifled a yawn—he was exhausted—and reminded Brent that revision was an integral aspect of the course, and that Brent had claimed to be willing to do additional work to bring up his grade.

"Yeah, but I already redid a different essay." Brent wagged his knees back and forth in a pair of oversized Payne sweatpants. Writing five hundred words every day, he said, was already a lot. And no one else was redoing that much of their work. He didn't see why someone in their group had gotten a good grade for writing about throwing up in the British Museum.

Fitger assured Brent that the other students (most of them; D.B. had reportedly taken the night train from Paris and was "catching some Z's" in his room) were working hard, and many of them had, in fact, been required to revise. (Fitger had forbidden Elwyn the use of exclamation points, banned Felicity from rhyme and alternative fonts, and asked Sonia to eliminate emoticons—and include a more accurate spelling, please, of the instructor's last name.) "If you want to improve your grades, you'll need to work hard and write more often," he said. "Even writing poorly—because you can always revise—is better than not writing at all."

"Yeah, but my poorly writing is worse than other poorly-people's writing," Brent said. "And getting an A for puking in the British Museum—"

Fitger held up his hand. Comparing grades with other students was not constructive, he said. And for what it was worth, successful writing often depended more on execution than subject. If the throwing up was relevant and skillfully rendered, it deserved a good grade.

Brent chewed up another handful of potato chips. If a student could write about vomit, he said, what else were they allowed to write about? Could they write about sex?

If it happened during the trip and had fewer than three grammatical errors, then, yes, Fitger said. "Now," he said. "Your revision. Let's see what you've got."

Brent sighed and offered up a wrinkled sheet of notebook paper, which Fitger smoothed out on the table in front of them. It was a bedraggled, handwritten document, and Brent's penmanship was large and disproportional, like the printing of a very young child.

To the guy at the scholarship office I don't remember his name. I am supposed to write a letter for an assignment from England. it is in the UK not my favorite place so far and because I didn't get a scholarship I will have to work extra hours over the summer. I am not saying this to make you an escape goat but I should not pay a price I can't effort to come to a country where it always rains. You gave my girlfriend Sonia the money. One another reason I don't like it here is they can't make a ½ decent sandwidge someone should teach them about the BLT (I would do it myself but that is not my roll)

Fitger gripped his red marking pen. "All right," he said. "First things first. Tell me what your main idea is. Just give me one. One central idea."

"You want some potato chips?" Brent tipped the bag toward him.

"No, thank you. One central idea."

Brent looked to the ceiling for inspiration. "I wish I could beat the shit out of that scholarship guy. And I can't tell if Sonia wants to be with me anymore. She isn't wearing my grandmother's ring. When I asked her if she was going to wear it she said she hasn't decided. I don't know what that means."

"I'm sure that's upsetting." Fitger brushed some salted crumbs from his legal pad. "But the status of your relationship may not belong in the same—"

"The thing is," Brent said, "me and Sonia used to be really tight. And it was like, we were the only ones we wanted to be with. And I know it wasn't right what I did—but it was just once, and I didn't even care about that other girl. She was really smart, though. I think she got an A in that class."

Fitger perused the rest of Brent's paper, which displayed a marked level of confusion about what a paragraph consisted of, and what it was for. He coaxed Brent through an outline. "Now: start on a fresh page," he said. "Write three or four short sentences for each of the points we've listed here."

Brent's facial expression suggested that Fitger had asked him to carry a load of rocks up a hill. But he tucked his tongue into the corner of his mouth and, making use of Fitger's legal pad, gripped his pen in his fist. Ten minutes later (while Fitger perused a week-old copy of the London *Times*), he was finished. "It's definitely better now," he said. "It definitely helps, doing an outline first. But you'll probably still find something I need to fix."

Fitger put on his glasses.

To the guy at the scholarship office. I will look up his name.

I am angry about my scholarship money. Which you wouldn't give. My anger is like a red hot iron or very sharp knife. You have never seen anger like this before. I would come to your office to beat the shit out of you but I am in England.

"I stuck to the anger part." Brent pointed to the page with a blunt-tipped finger. "And I cut it into paragraphs. One idea at a time, like you said."

"Yes, I see the paragraphs." Fitger skimmed to the end of the page. The letter was signed Very sincerely yours, from, Brent Schraft.

"Did you have a girlfriend when you were in college?" Brent asked.

Fitger's red pen hovered like a pendulum over the essay. "At times I did. Brent—"

"And did you get married to her? I would have bought Sonia a different ring if we were getting married. But I didn't think she was ready for that. That's why I gave her my grandmother's ring. Do you think I should have bought her a new one?"

"Brent, I'm not the right person to consult when it comes to relationship advice," Fitger said. "I'm divorced."

Brent funneled the remainder of the potato chips into his mouth, then tossed the bag into the trash. "My aunt and uncle got divorced. My mom wanted them to go to counseling but they wouldn't go, and my uncle ended up living in our garage for a while. He slept next to the mower."

"That sounds . . . unfortunate," Fitger said.

Brent agreed that it was. His uncle brought grass clippings into the house when he came in for meals. "Maybe you could talk to her. To Sonia." He lowered his voice and leaned toward Fitger. "You could tell her how it sucks being divorced—you know, how it's lonely being alone and divorced by yourself. And you could tell her you talked to me and you know I feel bad about my cheat, it was just for a grade, and then you could explain that people make mistakes but it's not a big deal." His knees continued to wag back and forth.

"Brent, it's not my place to get involved in—"

"I already told her I'm sorry and sometimes it seems like she forgives me but sometimes she still gets mad. And you know how to put things into words much better than me, so she'd understand if it came from you. If you could explain." He raked his hand through his hair. "Why did you get divorced? I mean, whose fault was it?"

"What?" Fitger had allowed his thoughts to drift toward the six-pack of beer in the mini-fridge in his room. "Does it always have to be somebody's fault?"

"Yeah, I think so," Brent said. "Or do you think what happened with me and Sonia was partly on her?"

Fitger suggested that their conversation stick to Brent's essay, but Brent said he would rather finish it by himself, at another time.

HAMPTON COURT PALACE: A CRITIQUE

BY LIN JEN SNOW

For some reason everything we do in England is about wealth, namely obscene amounts of money held by a very few people with no idea what real life consists of for the majority of the planet and no feelings of justice or accountability. Hampton Court Palace is the latest example. We are supposed to be impressed by Henry the Eighth spending his summers playing tennis and killing animals for sport. He used the palace mainly for parties and for getting ready to murder his wives (he built a gate for Anne Boleyn but cut off her head before it was finished). I would rather learn about the lives of people like my nai nai than about Henry with his necklaces and his leggings and the codpiece that he probably padded so his wives and mistresses would—

Fitger's phone lit up with a text. It was Janet, wanting to know if he was awake.

Of course he was awake. It was 1:00 a.m. but his sleep-addled brain seemed to think it was time for a nice hors d'oeuvre before dinner. He dialed her number, and she answered not with "hello" but by saying she knew he'd be up, he'd always had trouble with his circadian rhythm. Had he tried melatonin?

"I don't need it," he said. "I've decided to renounce all possibility of sleep until we get home." He told Janet that he would be making a suggestion regarding instructors for future Experience: Abroad classes, all of whom should be subject to fitness and stamina tests, able to do push-ups with their students at dawn.

"I don't remember push-ups ever being a part of your daily routine," Janet said. "Is the class going well?"

"I'm not sure it could be described that way," he said. "Why?"

"Just curious. A friend in the scholarship office told me that one of their staff got a menacing message on email this afternoon. Apparently someone in your group fulfilled an assignment by threatening to beat up a financial aid staffer. You may be hearing from one of the deans."

"Ah." Fitger sauntered into the kitchen and poured himself a cup of water; it had a rusty, unpleasant flavor. "That's Brent. And the message was supposed to be hypothetical; I didn't think he would send it." He told Janet about his student's romantic transgression: the disabled paramour, the deceased grandmother, and the ring of an undesirable color that had yet to make an appearance on Sonia's hand.

"Interesting," Janet said. "The email also mentioned something about the instructor of the class falling down a flight of stairs and spraining his ankle."

"Your concern is touching," Fitger said. "Is that why you called?"

Janet's response was indistinct. She asked about his other students. Were they getting along?

Hard to tell, Fitger said. But his impression was that no, in fact, they were not. Other than the inseparable twins, and apart from Brent's incessant yearning for Sonia, they had yet to coalesce as a group. It had been his plan, outside of classtime, to avoid them, but no matter how standoffish he strove to be, they sought him out to confide in him or ply him with questions. Was chicken considered meat? Did Fitger play poker, and did he have any chips? What was the second verse to the school song, "Oh Payne, Our Payne"? The only student he rarely spoke with was D.B., who, following a thorough talking-to regarding his unauthorized solo trip to Paris, had (Fitger was told) caught a flight to Madrid.

"Not that I blame him," Fitger said. It was such a relief, talking to Janet. She understood his need, on a regular basis, to unload and complain. "It hasn't even been a week yet," he told her. And they had three daylong bus trips ahead of them, the first one to Oxford the following morning. Trapped on a bus with eleven students! Well, ten, because D.B. would be quaffing sangria and eating tapas. Or, possibly, nine, because one of the students, Xanna, had a habit of getting sick and staying behind by herself in the dorm.

Janet tsked. "Did you take her to a doctor?"

"She hasn't been *that* sick," Fitger said. "I saw her at dinner a few hours ago, so I suppose she's recovered."

"You *suppose* she's recovered? You're a hypochondriac, Jay. You should ask her if she needs a doctor."

Fitger envisioned himself in an exam room, holding the trembling hand of a young woman in a paper gown. No: Xanna was fine. He set his cup of water in the sink and looked out the window. By the light of a streetlamp, two young lovers (perhaps his students; he couldn't see them well enough from a distance) were entwined in a concupiscent embrace. He suffered a momentary out-of-body detachment: he was one of the young lovers, kissing by the yellow light of the lamp, while some wintry Methuselah, from a window, observed.

"While we're on the topic of medical care," Janet said, "I told you I rescheduled Rogaine's appointment for the thirty-first. Did you write it down?"

"Of course I wrote it down." Fitger strode to his desk and opened his planner, noting that the thirty-first of the month was entirely blank. He picked up a pen and quickly wrote *dog*.

"He got into a fight with the corgi across the street yesterday," Janet said. "I hate that dog. *Patty*. Who names a dog Patty?"

Fitger dimly remembered Rogaine humping a foreshortened creature named Patty. "Perhaps it's a pseudonym." He returned to the window and looked out; the kissing couple was gone. On his ex-wife's end of the line, he heard the clatter of dishes. Janet still had the plates they'd used when they were married, white with a thin green stripe around the rim. She hadn't ended the call or hung up: strange. Janet didn't typically linger on the phone. "You wanted to know if I was awake," he said. "You texted. Was it only to tell me that I'm in for a scolding from the dean?"

He heard a sudden, thorough inhale. This was his ex-wife's tell. "I may need a letter from you after all," she said.

"Really." He felt a smile stretch across his face. "Might this be in reference to a job application?"

"You have no idea how much I hate to ask you this," she said.

"Oh, I can guess. And I'm happy to pause here for a moment while you search for the best way to phrase your request. You could start by saying that you know the letter of recommendation to be a form of discourse at which I have always—"

"Please shut up," she said, "and tell me you'll do it, and I'll let you know what the parameters are. There can be no innuendo, no clever puns, no mention of—"

"Yes. I accept. I will write you a letter of recommendation." Feeling a ripple of contentment, Fitger shuffled into the bedroom and lay down on the bed. He noticed a California-shaped stain on the ceiling. "I suppose you'd rather I not reference the many off-brand uses of whipped cream that during our early years together you—"

"Jay? Can you do this without being an ass? If you can't, I want you to say so."

He kept quiet.

"I must be out of my mind," Janet said. She would send him her résumé and a couple of paragraphs—a template, she explained—to start him off. His letter should be no longer than one or two pages, with no digressions. "And you have to show it to me before you send it."

"I never show candidates their letters."

"I'm not a 'candidate.' I'm your ex-wife, a fact that will go unmentioned in your letter, which isn't due until the end of next week. I'll send you something by email in a couple of days."

"Good. We'll be in touch, then." He heard Janet ask Rogaine to go fetch his leash. She had trained the dog to obey her in ways that he would never have obeyed Fitger. A snuffling noise and a jingling of tags suggested that she had set the phone down, probably to put on her coat and scarf and gloves. Fitger waited. In seven hours he would be on a bus en route to Oxford. He had a map of the city as well as a guidebook, but he hadn't yet read past the Norman Conquest. *Sixteen days left,* he thought.

"Janet? Are you there?"

The only answer was a continued jingling of tags and some canine breathing.

"Rogaine? Is that you?" Fitger asked. "This is your master speaking to you from England. You are an ugly, ugly dog, do you know that? Do you?"

Rogaine barked.

"That's right: ugly and malodorous," Fitger said. "Compared to other dogs, you're a—"

"Jay? Leave Rogaine alone," Janet said. "We're off for a walk."

SIX

The trip to Oxford began with Fitger in the role of lamp-lighter or town crier, knocking on doors to roust the under-grads from their beds. The Trout had told him that the bus would be ready to leave at 8:30 a.m. At 8:15, Lin was the only student who had emerged from her room in search of food.

"Are the others on their way?" he asked. "I was getting ready to check for a carbon monoxide issue in the second-floor hall."

Lin smeared a couple of slices of toast with strawberry jam. "We were out pretty late last night," she said. "Have you ever been to the Five Swans?"

Through the lobby doors, Fitger saw a squat white minibus pulling up to the curb. "The five . . ."

"Swans." Lin bit into the toast, a dollop of jam finding its way to her cheek. "It's the pub we've been going to. Kind of a dive. Some of the pubs here close at one, but the Swans stays open until three. The bartender knows us now, so that's cool."

"The bartender knows you? You've been here for *one week*." Fitger looked at his watch. "Is everyone being . . . safe and responsible?"

"Ha. Were you 'safe and responsible' at our age? Hang on,

I forgot: your generation is the one that treated the planet like a trash can and transferred ninety-nine percent of the wealth to people who only care about their own pleasure." Lin used the tip of her tongue, in a dexterous snake-like move, to recapture the jam.

Fitger waved to Elwyn and Joe Ballo, who had come down the stairs, carrying daypacks attached to water bottles. Undergrads, he had observed, carried water with them everywhere, as if expecting at any moment to find themselves crossing a desert. Fitger explained to Lin that he was referring to responsibility in more immediate terms. "I don't want anyone stumbling through the streets alone at night and getting mugged, or going to the hospital for overindulging." He lowered his voice. If she knew anything along those lines that he should be—

She froze him with a look, midsentence. "I'm not your narc." She gestured with her piece of toast. "It looks like that woman over there wants to talk to you."

Fitger turned. In the lobby doorway, a tall, severe-looking person with bulldog jowls and ash-gray hair in a painful-looking ponytail was talking to the driver of the minibus. "We leave in nine minutes," she said, when Fitger walked up.

The driver wandered away for a cigarette, and Fitger and the woman shook hands. Her name was Arva. She identified herself as his guide.

"My guide to what?" he asked.

She looked at him as if he were emitting an unusual smell. Herman Trout had made the arrangements, she said. She would go with him and his students to Oxford. Also, the following trips to Stonehenge and Bath.

"I wasn't told we needed a guide." He felt for his map of Oxford and realized that he had left it upstairs.

"You have been to Oxford many times?" Arva asked. "You know the city, upward and forth?"

"No, but—"

"And you have been as well to Bath? You learn its history? You can explain to your students what they will see?"

Brent and Xanna and Felicity had come downstairs. They were clearly eavesdropping on his conversation. "Well, if Herman Trout arranged for you to come with us, I suppose that's fine," Fitger said.

"We leave now in seven minutes." Arva tightened her ponytail and asked him what language he preferred she should speak with the students. She was born in Bucharest and raised in Aalborg, and she was fluent in Romanian, German, Russian, Danish, English, French . . .

"These are American Midwesterners," Fitger said. Anyone who spoke six languages fluently in the United States would be considered a diplomat or a genius; here, such verbal fluidity got you a part-time job as a guide.

"Six minutes," Arva said.

Fitger took his phone out of his pocket to text the students and found a message from D.B., consisting of a selfie taken not in Madrid, but on the Charles Bridge, in Prague.

Sitting at the front of the bus behind the driver, Fitger thought, would discourage interaction with the undergrads and allow him to get started on his recommendation letter for Janet. Though he had never worked with her at Payne, the law school being a sovereign institution, he had a fairly clear idea of her job and its responsibilities and could praise her intelligence, her tenacity, and her organizational skills. But those were generic qualities, and Fitger—now doodling in the margins of a small spiral notebook—knew that an effective reference letter was detailed and specific; it went beyond surface characteristics. Janet would probably want him to mention her computer skills, whatever those were, and her supervisory capability. (He remembered her overseeing—somewhat severely—his reorganization of their one-car garage.) He could, of course, eulogize her writing chops. Back in grad school, he remembered her working for months on a twelve-line poem—never published, as far as he knew—about some sort of bird.

To the Members of the Hiring Committee . . .

In the seats behind him, the students were playing balloon volleyball. Did Fitger want in on the game?

"Thank you, no." He clicked the tip of his pen. *This letter warmly recommends to you Janet Matthias, who has informed me that she is applying—*

A yellow balloon drifted into his line of vision. He batted it back. The word "warmly," he thought, was problematic. "Warm" was like "tepid." He would have to resort to the overused "enthusiastic." *This letter enthusiastically recommends to you—*

The balloon floated toward him.

"Spike!" someone shouted. With an elegant backhand, he sent the balloon spinning toward the rear of the bus.

—Ms. Janet Matthias, a candidate for your position, who has informed me that—

He doodled absently at the edge of the page. Why did the word "position" make it sound as if his ex were competing for second base on a softball team? The balloon glided back into view. Arva, in the seat across from him, plucked it from the air and squeezed it until it popped. "This is not appropriate," she said.

In the seats behind them, someone swore. Arva stood up and snapped her fingers.

Fitger had never seen anyone snap their fingers in such a menacing way. "All right, settle down, everyone," he said. He tucked his notebook into his pocket and turned toward the window: rain. He imagined moss beginning to grow beneath his arms.

As a tour guide, Arva was relentlessly efficient. She led the group on a forced march through the city of dreaming spires, through Christ Church Meadow and the botanical gardens, to the Carfax Tower and the covered market, the Bodleian Library and the Radcliffe Camera—and through the narrow courtyard of an historic pub where an American president famously sampled marijuana but did not inhale. But Fitger wondered how well she knew the city: she had a habit—it drove him nearly insane—of reciting at excessive volume what could easily be read on placards and signs.

In the early afternoon, they paused for lunch in a vault-cum-cafeteria with picnic-style tables. Fitger took a seat next to Wyatt, whose meal consisted of a large slice of cake and two tankards of beer. Fitger asked him if he had heard of vegetables.

"Ha! Yeah. They sound familiar," Wyatt said. He wiped his mouth with the back of his hand.

Fitger looked around to see where the other students were sitting. Brent and Sonia had tucked themselves into a corner, and the twins appeared to be quizzing Arva about Johannes Vermeer. Joe was in earnest conversation with a pair of nuns, and Xanna, Felicity, and Lin were sharing a table with a family, Lin engaging a dark-haired child in some sort of game.

And, at a narrow table near the bathrooms, Elwyn sat hunched over a plate of food by himself. He was wearing a black raincoat over a black shirt and black pants; he looked like the driver of a hearse. Fitger waved to him. "Elwyn—come and sit with us. Over here: we have plenty of room."

Elwyn sighed and stood and, with the air of a doomed man dragging himself toward his own execution, made his way toward Fitger and Wyatt. He set down his tray, which held a small glass of water and a plate with a pale slab of fish; it was the saddest meal Fitger had ever seen.

"So: What do you think of Oxford so far?" Fitger asked.

Elwyn stabbed a sallow bit of fish with his fork. He was disappointed, he said. He had assumed they would be visiting Oxford Castle. Once a prison and still the haunt of poltergeists, it was an odd omission from their tour.

Fitger submerged a spoon into his bowl of soup, hoping against hope that it wouldn't punish him later in the form of heartburn. "What about you, Wyatt? First impressions?"

Wyatt had finished his first tankard of beer and started in on the second. His appearance in the last few days was somewhat unkempt, his hair standing up in odd directions. "The weather sucks," he said. Then, looking at Elwyn: "What the heck is a poltergeist?" he asked.

Setting his plate of fish aside, Elwyn explained in detail the differences between phantoms, wraiths, banshees, djinns, spirits, and revenants. Fitger finished his soup—it would definitely wreak its vengeance later—and considered his recommendation for Janet. It was odd, he thought, that she hadn't given him details about the position she was applying for. He might know some members of the hiring committee, in which case the tone of his letter—

"We are ready to leave in five minutes." This was Arva, knocking the leg of her chair against Fitger's still bruised and tender shin. "We have three museums this afternoon."

"We just got here," Fitger said. "Some of the students are still eating." He told Arva that three museums sounded like at least one too many; he wanted to allow the undergrads a bit of free time.

"Then you and I can have a head start. We will visit the ATM." Arva tightened her ponytail.

"The ATM," Fitger repeated.

"Yes. For my payment." She named a sum.

But: Wasn't Herman Trout paying her?

No, the Trout made the appointment, Arva said, but the payment was Fitger's, and cash was preferred. "I will make up a bill and the rest is for you to discuss with your university."

Fitger reached for his wallet. He would submit a receipt for Arva's services to Payne's Experience: Abroad office, but he had little hope of ever seeing that money again.

.   .   .

After lunch, they walked down Turl Street to the History of Science Museum to peruse its collection of fifteenth-century sundials, elaborate orreries and astrolabes, and armillary spheres. Arva read aloud from a pamphlet handed to her by a docent, and then announced that the students had thirty minutes to explore the exhibits; they would be leaving for their next museum in half an hour.

Fitger made a circuit of the first floor, gazing through tempered glass at a silver-encrusted microscope that must have weighed at least forty pounds. Joe Ballo drew his attention to a marble Ouija board. "It's a holy table. That's what it's called," Joe said. "It's written in the language that angels speak."

Fitger wondered aloud what sort of conversation one would have with an angel, should the opportunity ever occur.

"It's just superstition." Joe had a habit of scowling while collecting his thoughts, his filigreed eyebrows pulling toward each other like two sides of a drawbridge. "But I used to try to talk to my mom with a Ouija board. I didn't think she could hear but I still did it. I felt like I should try. You know?"

Fitger's phone rang in his pocket.

"I kept a lock of her hair after she died," Joe Ballo said. "I told myself that it still smelled the way she used to smell, but maybe that wasn't true. I don't think I remember her smell anymore. I had the hair saved in an envelope, but my aunt threw it out. She thought it was trash. That's what she told me, anyway. I went out back and looked through the cans but it was gone."

Fitger's phone continued to ring; he thought of D.B. in a jail cell in Prague. "Joe, I'm sorry, I need to get this." He stepped aside to answer. "Yes? Hello?"

"Jay! I've been trying to reach you." Fitger recognized the phlegm-inflected voice of Albert Tyne, a semi-demented colleague at Payne. Tyne was known for his slovenly appearance and feculent habits, and he occupied his office in Willard Hall like a bear in a cave. "This goddamn copy machine isn't working."

"I'm not on campus right now, Albert." Fitger watched Joe Ballo ambling away from the Ouija board to contemplate a set of Napier's bones. "Who gave you this number?"

"The feeder keeps jamming," Tyne said. "I can't find anything stopping it up. I've put the paper in the slot the way it tells me to. And I've pushed the reset button several times, but—"

"I'm in London, Albert. Or, actually, Oxford. You need to ask Fran about the copier. But whatever you do, don't take the tray out."

Albert suggested that perhaps he should take the tray out.

"Do not take the tray out," Fitger said. *"Do you hear me, Albert? Do not—"*

"Damn," Tyne said. "The tray fell apart. And now there are metal bits all over the—"

Fitger stuffed the phone in his pocket. It was time for their next museum.

During the short walk down the street, the cold dripping down the back of his collar, Fitger fielded two more calls from his colleague at Payne. Tyne continued wreaking havoc in the copy room; having disabled the Xerox machine, he'd moved on to the fax. Fitger ultimately persuaded him to abandon his efforts—without touching any other piece of equipment, including the hole punch and the stapler—and followed up with an admonitory SOS to Fran, ending his message by asking her how things in the department, other than Albert Tyne, might be going. Fran's answer consisted of an animated video of a sinking ship, complete with cartoon passengers waving their arms.

Museum #2, the Pitt-Rivers, was an unusual choice, Fitger thought, resembling a mentally unstable person's neglected storage unit or abandoned garage. He meandered through collections of musical instruments made from seashells, clothing sewn from animal intestines, and ancient coins, shoes, weapons, boats, headdresses, prophylactic devices, and skull-trepanning tools. After squinting into an ill-lit display case that featured hexes, fetishes, and a witch in a small silver flask, he headed to the men's room, alert to the smoldering effects of the soup he'd ingested at lunch. Later, on his way to the exit, he was intercepted by Elwyn, who had discovered a collection of shrunken heads.

"I've read about these but never saw them before," he said. Typically dour, Elwyn glowed with ebullience. "They take the skull out," he explained. "They break the skull bones and pull them out in pieces through the severed neck. That's how the heads get smaller. Then, going back through the neck, they put a placeholder inside—probably a stone—to keep the round shape, and after they sew the lips and the eyes shut, they boil the—"

"Elwyn? Let me just say this up front: you're not going to write your five hundred words about these heads."

Elwyn gestured zealously toward the display case. He was so thin—a skeletal framework, Fitger thought, in funeral clothes.

"You told us we could write about anything we saw today," he said. "You told us that—"

"Yes, I know what I told you. But you and I have talked about branching out. Trying something that isn't . . . macabre. A different topic and tone."

"I could do research about the heads," Elwyn suggested. "I could find out if the people who shrunk them were—"

"Elwyn? No. Not this time," Fitger said. "Find something else."

On the sidewalk when they emerged from the museum—it had stopped raining, and the students stood with their startled faces upturned toward the light—Fitger was distracted by a woman who cut through their group. Her hair was pinned to the back of her head in a way that Janet used to wear hers, and she made her way through them balletically, swiveling her shoulders. He experienced a shimmer of déjà vu: Janet cutting in front of him, impatient, on a city sidewalk, the peppermint smell of her shampoo tinting the air and the back of her neck close enough that he could admire—as he often did—the cup-like hollow at the top of her spine.

"What a surprise!" someone said. "Running into Jason Fitger in Oxford."

It took Fitger a moment to recognize the person who had materialized in front of him: Thor Markusen, former colleague, a slender, unctuous man with an otter's physique, dressed in a rakish black gown like an Oxford don. Thor—whose name must have been bestowed ironically, or as an act of wishful thinking—used to teach philosophy at Payne, but after writing a book called *Awkward: Understanding Discomfort in Human Interactions* (a simplistic work, ridiculed by everyone Fitger knew until it became an international bestseller) he was transformed, unexpectedly, into a star. Fitger suspected that Thor and Janet had once had an affair.

They shook hands while Arva and the undergrads looked on.

So! Fitger was leading a *study-abroad program,* Thor said. He was still teaching, then? *And these were his distinguished young scholars from Payne University?* Thor adopted an expression of bemused sympathy, Fitger noting his former colleague's annoying habit of bowing almost imperceptibly while appearing to speak in italics. He was tempted to ask if Thor regularly practiced his new British accent in front of a mirror. Instead, he inquired as to whether Thor was still teaching.

No, no, no, no, no, no, no, no. Thor wasn't teaching—that is, *not teaching per se:* he was a visiting fellow at All Souls, which, as Fitger probably knew, was *one of the oldest and most prestigious of the Oxford colleges.* It was just across Holywell Street, across from the Radcliffe Camera. He would have invited Fitger to dinner—*the high table, you know*—if he'd had some warning, but without notifying the All Souls manciple in advance, it wasn't possible; these things, *at least at All Souls College, as Fitger surely must understand,* just weren't done.

Fitger listened to Markusen rattle on and wondered how many times he could fit the words "All Souls" into each sentence. Had Janet actually gone to bed with this cretin? Fitger would have to talk to her about raising her standards. "We don't want to detain you, Thor," he said. "We go back to London in a few hours, and—"

"Oh, yes. Yes, of course." Thor smiled. Fitger *and his entourage* needed to make the most of their time and see as much of Oxford as possible. Had they visited one of the colleges? No? Well, perhaps they'd enjoy a private tour of All Souls. Nothing exhaustive, but Thor could show them the chapel—built in the early 1400s—as well as the courtyards, the historic quadrangle with the sundial designed by Christopher Wren . . .

Fitger tried to refuse. He turned to Arva. They were on a schedule, weren't they? They didn't want to miss the, uh, the . . . ?

"No," Arva said. "We would enjoy to have this tour."

For the next ninety minutes, Fitger endured his former colleague's benevolence. All Souls College, Thor explained, his black gown billowing picturesquely behind him, was founded by the Archbishop of Canterbury in the 1400s; unique among the Oxford colleges, it had no graduate or undergraduate students. Undergrads were briefly admitted in the 1500s *as servants* (Thor indulged, here, in an ingratiating little chuckle), but this practice was eventually stopped. He led the students into the chapel and around the immaculate quads, all while describing the college's superb collection of silver and its famous wine cellar. Though not the wealthiest of the thirty-nine associated colleges, its endowment was in the four hundred millions. Nothing in Oxford, Thor explained, could compare to All Souls.

The students were noticeably impressed. Sonia asked Thor about his black gown.

"You want to know why I'm not *in mufti?*" Thor bared a set of chipped teeth and explained that the gown was tradition. It served as an insignia: those who wore it were recognized and respected as members of the university. "Your professor Fitger probably wears such a gown on occasion, but of course Payne—*if I remember it correctly*—is a little less formal." He nodded in acknowledgment of two passing scholars, one of whom Fitger recognized as a winner of the Nobel Prize. "Academe: It's a life of constant endeavor. Always a challenge." He laid a manicured hand on the sleeve of Fitger's jacket. "Have you been working on anything new? Are there any novels in the pipeline? I don't believe I've seen your name in the reviews in the past few years. I hope I haven't missed anything."

"You'll be the first to know, Thor, when I publish another book. I'll hope for half the undeserved attention that your work has received."

Brent turned to Fitger. "You wrote a book?"

"He wrote a number of books," Thor said. "Novels. They may be difficult to find in stores nowadays, but perhaps he has one at home, in a closet." He accompanied the group to the gate and leaned toward Fitger, his breath smelling of cheese. "Give my regards to Janet, won't you?"

The gate clicked shut between them, Fitger managing, between gritted teeth, to thank Thor for the tour.

With only ninety minutes left until they had to return to the bus, Fitger overruled Arva's plan to sprint through a thousand years of art, history, and culture at the Ashmolean Museum and granted the undergrads the rest of the afternoon to roam the cobbled streets of Oxford before meeting at five o'clock for the ride back to London and the dorm. He watched them scatter like pinballs—Elwyn in the direction of the haunted prison—and set off on his own, narrowly avoiding a pair of Jehovah's Witnesses and their cheery predictions of the end of the world.

Any novels in the pipeline? Thor's unguinous voice tunneled into his mind like a worm. Here was a pseudo-scholar who had written one book and had spent the years since its publication overseeing reprints and inspirational posters featuring selections from its insipid pages. Fitger had published five novels. Five! They were all out of print, sinking like stones beneath the surface of public attention, but he had put his mind and his heart and his sweat into every sentence. It was demoralizing: the deafening silence that had greeted his last two books had taken a toll, and in the wake of their failure he had committed himself to that academic rest home—administration. He was slowing down. His imagination, once nimble, was beginning to ossify, bits of it slipping down the firepole of his brainstem from lack of use.

At the corner of a cobbled street, he came upon a pub called the Bear, a seventeenth-century watering hole with a remarkably low ceiling and framed rows of neckties on the walls and over his head. He ordered a pint and sat down. If Janet had had an affair with Thor, it probably would have occurred after her relationship with her tennis coach and before—or during?—her fling with the associate dean. Fitger kept track, without necessarily meaning to do so, of her liaisons, which were numerous but of short duration. While sipping his beer, he took his notebook, with the beginnings of his recommendation letter, from his coat pocket. Trying not to think about his stagnant literary career or about Thor, he set down his glass and picked up his pen. He would start afresh and write quickly. *Dear colleagues & committee members. It is w/ sincere enthusiasm and pride that I send this letter in regard to Ms. Janet—*

Good god, what was the word "pride" doing there, making his ex-wife sound like a ten-year-old at a piano recital? Oh well: he would revise later. The immediate goal was to get the words out.

—that I send this letter in regard to Ms. Janet Matthias, whom I know quite well and would be happy to vouch for in formal or informal contexts.

Fitger tore out the page.

"Hey there, Prof." Brent and Wyatt were coming toward him, carrying two pints of beer. Brent swaggered bowlegged in front, with Wyatt, limber and imperturbable, behind. Did Fitger mind if they sat with him? Cool. Why did he suppose the British served peanuts in their pubs but never popcorn? Was he writing something? No? What did he think about all the neckties on the walls—weird, huh? Like somebody killed off a whole bunch of kids. Also, wasn't it amazing that they ran into his friend from Payne on the street? Had Professor Fitger ever taught at Oxford?

Putting his notebook away, Fitger speculated about the penalty, if any, for day-drinking with students. "No," he said.

"It's probably hard to get a job there," Brent said. "You know, at Old Souls. But I guess you could get one if you didn't want to teach at Payne." He clinked his glass against Wyatt's and then against Fitger's. "You should have told us you wrote a book. What was it, a mystery?"

"Not really."

"Sonia likes mysteries," Brent said. "Me and Wyatt were just talking about her."

Wyatt shrugged. He had already downed half of his beer.

"I think she just read one," Brent said. "Sonia, I mean. I don't remember what it was called. Something about the woods. Dark woods, thick woods, something like that." He cracked a peanut open by crushing it against the table with the flat of his hand. "Wyatt thinks I should buy her a necklace. You know, instead of the ring."

"That's your deal," Wyatt said. "Whatever you think."

"You've got an opinion," Brent said. "You think I should get her something new. Either a bracelet or necklace."

"Not getting involved," Wyatt said. "It's all good."

Brent went to work on the rest of the peanuts. New jewelry was usually cheap next to the heirloom kind. Didn't Fitger agree? And Brent's grandmother's ring was definitely an heirloom. What was Fitger's opinion about the best kind of gift—you know, for a girl? A girlfriend. Had he ever bought something really nice, a really good gift, back when he was married? Something his wife really liked?

Wyatt finished his beer. "You were married?"

"I was," Fitger said. "Is that surprising?"

"Hey, it's none of my business." Wyatt stood up. He asked if anyone else wanted another beer.

"Maybe you should make it a soda this time." Fitger raised his voice to be heard above the laughter at a table behind them. "Or order some food. You seem to be doing a lot of drinking."

"Yeah, it's legal here," Wyatt said. "I use a fake ID at home."

Fitger pretended not to hear this; he offered to purchase some fish and chips.

Brent said he could eat some fish and chips.

"I'll buy two orders," Fitger said, "if Wyatt sits down."

Halfway to the bar, Wyatt paused and looked at his feet—at his recently purchased and now thoroughly wet overpriced sneakers—and Fitger understood that he had shamed his student.

"Come on, Wyatt," Brent said. "I'm hungry. You can get a drink in London later."

Wyatt sat, and Fitger placed an order for two fish-and-chips. "Enjoy!" he said, with a note of false cheer. He would see them on the bus, he said, in an hour.

The rain started up again as soon as he left the pub. The entire country, Fitger thought, had the climate of a kitchen sponge. He headed toward the parking lot with a nap on the bus in mind, but when he climbed aboard, wet through his clothes, he saw a passenger already seated. It was *F for Feline = Felicity*.

She waved to him by wiggling her fingers. "I got here early," she said. "I was afraid I wouldn't be able to find my way back."

Fitger took off his coat and sat nearby, across the aisle. Wasn't she in a group with Xanna and Lin?

"I was; but they walk really fast," she said. "And I think they might have forgot I was with them. Look: I bought some postcards. But I should have remembered about stamps. I don't know if the store where I bought these sold any stamps,

I should have asked. And I got these little lemon candies." She lifted the lid from a tin. "You don't want one? Whoosh! They're sour." She flipped through her postcards and moved to the edge of her seat, to be closer to Fitger. "I'm not going to mail all of these. Some are for me. I'm going to keep them. Look at this one. Look at the queen and her little corgis! Their legs are so small. I wish they wouldn't dock their tails; I think that's cruel." She continued to rustle through her belongings. Oxford was interesting, she said, and so different from Payne. Everything was so old! It was good to travel and to see things. Still, it was hard to be away from home. But she wouldn't think about that now, because she had to plan out her assignment of five hundred words. She liked the prompt he had given them, about the tangible and intangible things they'd brought with them to England. She'd had to look up the word "intangible"; she hoped that was okay. She used to work on vocabulary in grade school, but it seemed like no one did that anymore.

Did Fitger think it would be a good idea—or would it be stupid—if she wrote about the sweater she was wearing? Because the sweater was a tangible thing, and she got it for Christmas. She had to roll up the sleeves—see?—because they were too long. The *intangible* thing she wanted to write about was being shy. It was hard to describe why she thought of those two things the same way, and she knew the professor liked it when they explained and described things, but all she could think of was that being shy was like a sweater that didn't quite fit, because it covered you and people looked at it and you worried that maybe they could see something wrong. The other kids from the trip all lived in dorms, but—probably the professor didn't know this—Felicity lived with her mother a mile from campus. Her mother supervised one of the dining halls at Payne and sometimes they ate breakfast or even dinner together there. People complained about the dining hall food, but Felicity thought it was good, most of the time. Her mother worked really hard.

Thanks, no, that was nice of him, but she was okay. Sometimes she just thought about things at home and missed them and she felt really sad. She was going to work on her assignment now. But first she would quickly check email, because her mother had promised to send more photos of their cat, Mrs. Gray. Look, here they were! Did Professor Fitger want to see them? Here was the window where Mrs. Gray liked to sit, so she could look at the birds. Look how nice her fur was! Some long-haired cats, when they aged, had trouble with bald spots or mats, but Mrs. Gray's coat, which Felicity usually brushed every day with a fine-tooth comb, was still really soft. Mrs. Gray wasn't a purebred, but she was probably part Persian because her muzzle was short. See? Here was a close-up. Look. Wasn't she pretty? Both her under- and overcoat remained as thick and plush as they had ever been.

SEVEN

A SCOTCH EGG

BY SONIA MORALES (THIS IS MY FOOD REVIEW
OF SOMETHING I ATE IN ENGLAND, SORRY IT IS LATE
I HAVE HAD A LOT GOING ON)

For my food critic review of something I ate in England I will write about the Scotch egg which is a food you can usually find here in a bar. It is a weird and particular British food and to be honest I wasn't sure I wanted to eat one (I can be picky about what I eat) but for me this trip is about stretching myself and doing new things so I decided to do it because like the saying goes now is the time. We were a group of people in the pub near the dorm called The Five Swans. I said, "Sonia, you will eat that egg," and so I did.

It is hard to describe a flavor because I am used to describing what something looks like but not how the way it tastes on my tongue. I will describe it as salty and crumbly on the outside and tasting like bacon, and even though hard boiled eggs are not my favorite it wasn't bad. I also liked the way it looked like wrappings of layers around the egg and thinking about how the restaurant must of cooked it I said mostly thinking to myself but it was out loud that it reminded me of a ship in a bottle, because how did the egg get inside of all that crust?

Brent was sitting next to me not in a good mood, he said they just wrap the bacon around. I still wish he wasn't apart of this trip, he is always staring at my hands to see if I am wearing his grandmother's ring. (Which it isn't my birthstone or not the style of ring I would buy.) Anyway it turns out he was wrong about the bacon, because Joe Ballo was sitting across from us and has worked in restaurants and he said it wasn't bacon, it was sausage and pork. He said you take a hard-boiled egg and roll it in ground pork and then in breadcrumbs, then you fry it in oil. Or you can bake it (he said) but some people don't think that's as good because people like oil.

Usually the guys (Brent and Wyatt) leave Joe alone because he is a little older and maybe killed someone, but Brent got a hair up his ass, he ordered wontons and was trying to write a paper about them. He asked Joe Ballo if his middle name was Betty F. Crocker.

Joe said that depended, because what was the F for?

I thought that was funny but Brent was already in a bad mood and he picked up the rest of my Scotch egg and squeezed it hard in his fist. He asked me when we met in front of the bathrooms (he had to wash his hands because of the egg) if I had a thing for Joe Ballo or maybe hooked up with him. I said if I was going to hook up with someone it wasn't going to be Joe and it wasn't Brent's business anyhow.

Brent wanted to know who I would hook up with but I wouldn't say.

I am not sure why I said that about hooking up with some-one. To be honest I have felt kind of confused during this trip, I am asking myself a lot of questions like why am I not as jealous anymore (Wyatt knows the girl from our Chem 101 he said she had to amputate her leg from cancer) and if I am not as jealous does that mean I don't care? Maybe I was with Brent because my mother liked him and we were used to each other but when I write that down I think I don't even know who I'm supposed to be anymore or even know who I am.

So that is the story of the Scotch egg which for me was something new that I tried. It was not bad as unusual foods might go but I don't think I will eat one again.

"If you're looking for sympathy," Janet said, "you've dialed the wrong number. We got two feet of snow here over the weekend, and you're being paid to sightsee with a Swedish guide."

"Danish," Fitger said. "Or Romanian. But I'm not convinced that she's really a guide. And I'm told that I'm stuck with her for the trips to Stonehenge and Bath." He could hear Janet typing. It was 11:00 p.m. in London, and therefore the end of the workday at Payne. She wouldn't typically have picked up a call from her ex while she was at work, but she had sent him her résumé and a template for her letter of recommendation a few hours before and was eager to know that they'd been received.

"You're almost halfway through the trip," she said. "Just over a week and a half left."

He hoped she didn't think this would cheer him. A week and a half was an eternity, he said. He would rather be flogged or drawn and quartered. He would rather—

"The self-pity is always entertaining," Janet said. "But let me interrupt this familiar aria to ask if you've looked at the template I sent."

"Yes, I looked at it." Fitger put his phone on speaker and walked into his mini-kitchen, opened the mini-fridge, and popped the metal cap from a beer. "It was more of a Mad Lib than a template. You gave me the choice of two different adjectives and two or three nouns. I'm writing a letter, not a fill-in-the-blank."

"I'm trying to save you some time," Janet said. "It's called efficiency."

"It's not efficiency if I have to completely rewrite the whole thing. Your version is flat. It doesn't sound like me."

"I don't want it to sound like you," Janet said. "I want it to sound like it was written by a sane and balanced person who . . . Hang on." He heard her saying goodbye to a colleague.

When she picked up the phone again, he told her not to worry about the letter. He would get it written; he was a writer, wasn't he? "It's no problem at all," he said. "I'll squeeze it in over here, between crises." He told her about his latest undergraduate encounter, an impromptu tête-à-tête with Sonia in the dorm's basement laundry room. Sonia was disappointed with her grade on the Scotch egg essay—and, while emptying a brightly colored festival of underthings into the wash, she solicited Fitger's opinion: If one person in a relationship got to hook up with someone else, shouldn't the other person be allowed to do the same?

He turned the light off in his kitchen and tipped back his beer. "I'm beginning to feel like an advice columnist," he said, before describing some of the other students' recent essays: the twins' illustrated comparison of four different English biscuits, and the "Conversation with a Stranger" assignment, Felicity claiming to have met, in Trafalgar Square, a "really mean Mickey Mouse." The students seldom followed instructions: Elwyn had put his own twist on the "Conversation with a Stranger" idea, writing about an encounter between a kraken and a wyvern, which ended with a pair of hobnailed boots full of blood.

"Wait," Janet said. "How did you answer the student's question?"

"What question?"

"Your student in the laundry room, Jay! About the hookup! Oh, forget it. Never mind; I don't want to know."

"Hold on; don't hang up yet," Fitger said. "You'll never guess who the students and I saw when we were in Oxford."

"Let me try: Thor Markusen."

Fitger coughed. "Did I already tell you that?"

"No. Thor called and told me."

"I didn't realize that you were in touch with him."

"We talk or email now and then. Did he tell you about the fellowship they've given him?" Janet proceeded to repeat to Fitger Thor's account of his time at All Souls. "And they don't have students," she said. "A college with a massive endowment and no students. Thor and the other faculty have lunch and dinner together and say important things, I suppose, while they pass the potatoes. Thor said they have a silver service at the high table and a wine cellar that—"

"Yes, yes, I heard all about the wine cellar," Fitger said. "Fortunately, Thor was an egotistical prig even before they gave him the fellowship, so it's possible the experience won't go to his head."

Janet suggested that it might be time for Fitger to get over the fact that Thor—and not Fitger—had published a best-seller. "He invited me to come visit him."

"Ha! Does he know how you feel about England?"

"He has a house in Italy," Janet said. "Outside Sienna. With a heated pool."

The image of Janet and Thor against a backdrop of olive trees and vineyards began to assume an unfortunate shape in Fitger's head.

On Janet's end of the line, he heard the sound of metal file cabinets opening and closing: she was probably getting her gloves and snow boots out of a drawer. She told him to let her know when his recommendation letter was finished.

Of course, he said. But: Would she remind him of the deadline?

"It's in the email."

"Right," Fitger said.

"And on the template. And I sent you a text. Enough: I'm going home."

"Wait," he said. He was just curious: Did she still happen to have the gold earrings he had given her? The ones that looked like little gold bells?

Janet didn't answer right away. "I don't know," she said. "Why?"

It wasn't important. One of the students had asked him if he had ever given a woman a gift of jewelry, and he seemed to remember that she had liked and worn the little bells, but he might have been wrong.

"I'm sure you're not talking to your students about me, or about our divorce," Janet said.

"No, of course not. No. That would be inappropriate."

"That's right. It would. Now I have to go home, so I can let the dog out. You're not going to screw this up for me, are you, Jay? You'll write the letter and send it?"

Yes. She had no call to doubt him. He would write the letter, and he would not screw it up.

WRITE ABOUT A SIGNIFICANT HISTORICAL FIGURE
(I DIDN'T LIKE THE CHOICES IN THE MUSEUM
SO I DID SOMETHING ELSE)

—BY LIN JEN SNOW

The statue of Boadicea and her daughters in a chariot—
sculpted by someone named Thornycroft—sits above eye level
at the end of the Westminster Bridge. Boadicea was queen of
the Iceni warriors in about the year 60, a group who fought the
Roman army, killing around 80,000 people and generally kick-
ing ass until the Romans came back and defeated them. Part of
the reason Boadicea is famous isn't her fighting skills but the
fact that she was raped, which is something men like to see
women be famous for. They think of raping a woman the way
a dog thinks about pissing on somebody's lawn.

Fitger took off his glasses and pinched the bridge of his nose.
"Please don't knock anyone's teeth out," he said.

Lin, while waiting for him to read her essay, was engaged
in a vigorous floor-hockey game (two brooms and a pair of
rolled-up socks that served as a puck) with one of the twins.

"Ms. Snow, did you hear me? Ms. Wagner-Hall?"

"We heard you. Backhand!" The balled-up socks sailed past
his head.

It's hard to see Boadicea's daughters from pavement level but
when you look at the statue online you can see they're behind

her and look afraid, both of them with bare breasts because artists always show women's breasts in sculptures even if the women are just walking the fucking dog or driving a fucking minivan to the grocery store.

Fitger circled the second instance of *fucking* and wrote "redundancy?" in the margins, then crossed it out.

"Cheap shot!" the twin called. "You know that's a foul."

"No foul. That's seven to one." Lin whooped after each goal—a nerve-piercing sound.

The remainder of her essay veered off into a discussion of vaginas being treated as foreign territories to be claimed and exploited by men. A few syntactical flaws, yes: but he wasn't eager to debate the argument's specifics.

The bristles of a broom raked his leg. "Game over. Have a seat, Ms. Snow, and let's talk about consistency and organization."

Lin propped her broom against the wall and flung herself into a chair. There was something fascistic, she said, about the way he was always hammering them on organization. Did he know that the concepts of thesis and argumentation were gendered? Was Fitger asking her to adhere to patriarchal standards that—

"Topic sentences." Elwyn had emerged from the room across the hall, wearing what looked like a gentleman's dressing gown and matching slippers, towel over his arm, on his way to the shower. "That's how you organize an essay."

"Fuck off, Vincent Price," Lin said.

Elwyn flinched.

Fitger closed his eyes while the bathroom room door

squealed shut, and then suggested that Lin might want to adopt a gentler tone with her fellow students. There were eleven more days of the trip in front of them, during which they needed to function as a group, and—

"Yeah, okay, I get it, I don't need the whole speech." Lin toyed with the socks that she had knotted into a puck. "But sometimes I can't help it. Some of these people are really getting on my nerves. You know?"

Fitger knew.

"We're together *all day*," Lin said, "and I try to stay cool and mind my own business, but it's impossible *not* to know who hooked up with who—"

Whom, Fitger thought.

"—and who wanted to lay down drunk in the street—"

Lie down, Fitger thought.

"—and, you know, most of the time I could care less—"

Couldn't care less.

"—if someone ditches class to go to Istanbul"—was D.B. in Istanbul? Fitger wondered—"but I don't have enough of my own space over here, so it pisses me off. I mean, I'm not hanging out in my room watching TV and half-assing this course. And I'm not jerking the instructor around. Doesn't it piss you off?" She picked up her essay, emblazoned with Fitger's red suggestions. "What is it called when you hate human beings?"

"Misanthropy," Fitger said.

"Yeah, I think that's what I've got. At least it's not catching."

Fitger told her that in fact it might be. He suggested that they return to Boadicea and her bare-breasted daughters at the edge of the Thames.

112

XANNA BLYTHE

NATIONAL PORTRAIT GALLERY ASSIGNMENT

Alexander Pope (1688-1744) appears in a 1737 painting by Jonathan Richardson. It has to be said: Pope looks like crap. His skin gleams in a way that you could attribute to inspiration, but something about the liquid shimmer in his eyes spells trouble. Did he look this bad in real life?

The painting is oil on canvas, 24 by 18. Pope is in profile and for some reason he's wearing a crown of bay leaves—wrong century for that accessory, my friend.

Wikipedia, authority on every person, place and subject, tells us that "As a child Pope survived being once trampled by a cow," which is something most people can't claim, also as an adult he was only four and a half feet tall, with a hunchback and rickets and tuberculosis and asthma and chronic headaches, not to mention "inflamed eyes."

The poor rickety slob. I'm no doctor but I see those eyes and I think, scleritis. He was probably in pain most of the time. He probably hated to walk up a flight of stairs.

N.B. Sorry this isn't finished. I kind of lost interest. And I wasn't feeling great and had to leave early for some R & R at the dorm.

Dreading the two-hour journey to Stonehenge and determined to keep the undergrads occupied during the trip,

Fitger announced, as the minibus lumbered away from the dorm and ran over a curb, that the students should use the next one hundred and twenty minutes to come up with a topic for their final essay. This longer, more formal paper would be due the day before they left England and was the culmination of the three-week term. He expected each student to get out their notebook and be able to show him a working thesis by the end of the day.

"You want us to do this *now?*" Brent asked. "While we're driving?"

Fitger pointed out that, thankfully, Brent was not the one behind the wheel.

For the first half hour, the ten students (D.B. was probably on his way to Vladivostok) fell gratifyingly silent. Across the aisle, Arva pulled a sleep mask over her eyes; soon a whistling sound came from her nose. Fitger opened his notebook and turned to his recommendation for Janet. He'd been drafting it piecemeal over the past few days. He skimmed his most recent effort, which included a reference to Janet's unconventional sense of humor and her facility with languages, including Pig Latin. He crossed this part out; a few minutes later, he scribbled *STET* at the edge of the page.

"Professor?" Joe Ballo, seated a few rows behind him, had a question. The syllabus described their final assignment as a "personal essay," and Joe—making use of his eyebrows for emphasis—wanted to know how personal the project should be.

Mentally reviewing the papers that some of the students had already written, which included information most people might reserve for the therapist's couch or the confessional or even the grave, Fitger explained that the goal was insight rather than intimacy; the choice of topic, as long as it related to their experiences and their thoughts while in England, was their own. Had Joe chosen a topic?

Yes. Mystery. He wanted to write about things that would never be known or understood.

"Interesting," Fitger said. As a topic, however, "mystery" sounded a bit broad. Could Joe Ballo possibly—

Elwyn chimed in. He liked the idea of mystery, too. He'd originally wanted to write his final paper about the Café in the Crypt, a tourist attraction near Trafalgar Square. But the crypt had proved disappointing; it was well lit and clean, and the sandwich he had eaten there was a little bit stale.

One of the twins wanted to know if Elwyn had eaten lunch in a funeral home.

No; a funeral home would have been more interesting, Elwyn said.

Fitger told them to reread the instructions on the syllabus. *In a work environment, Ms. Matthias exhibits all the requisite* . . .

Sonia complained of something slimy on the back of her seat.

Fitger crossed out *exhibits* (why did the word make him think about primates?) and then the whole phrase.

Brent stood in the aisle beside him. He had an idea for his final essay.

"All right."

"Charles Dickens."

Fitger waited for him to continue.

"He was a writer," Brent said.

Yes. Fitger had heard of him—and had in fact read about

115

him very recently, in Brent's "National Portrait Gallery" assignment, which had focused on a painting of Dickens as a young man. Brent had described Dickens as the author of many novels as well as the movie *Oliver!*, which he had watched with Sonia in her parents' basement at least three or four times. Following a brief physical description (Dick has a widows peek), Brent had dedicated most of his essay to the viewing of Sonia's favorite musical (she always sang along to the "ooom-pop-pop" song) and to the fact that he loved her and needed her to love him as she had before.

Fitger had given the paper a generous C, suggesting that Brent set Sonia and his grandmother and her ring aside and find a fresh topic. "You've already written about Dickens," he said, as Brent squeezed onto the seat by his side. Wouldn't Brent prefer to tackle something new, a significant moment or experience in England that he would remember and think back on in future years?

"Yeah, that's what I'm talking about," Brent said. "Because that paper made me think that I want to have a future career as a writer."

"Really." Fitger tried to adopt an attitude of polite interest.

"Yeah. And that's part of my experience in England." Fitger might be surprised to hear this, but he—Brent—had done some research about Dickens and how much he wrote. Like, he wrote *all the time*. Which had made Brent think about how much he and the other students in class were writing now, and how much better their writing was getting. And Brent's papers were definitely improving: Fitger had to agree that every essay he turned in was a little bit better than the essay before.

Fitger noticed a crust of dried blood on the tip of Brent's chin. "It takes a lot of time and effort to—"

"Oh, I know. You don't have to tell *me* that." Brent laughed. He knew that writing books and getting them published was probably hard, and he might not make a lot of money, at least not at first, but he had a lot of good ideas, really good ones, and that was the important part, wasn't it?

Across the aisle, Arva lifted her sleep mask and squinted in Fitger's direction.

"Our advisers at Payne are always telling us to look for mentors," Brent said. "And I figure you could be my mentor."

"That's something we could talk about. Eventually," Fitger said.

Arva pulled her mask back down.

Brent wanted to shake hands with him. They shook hands. It was good to have a goal, Brent said, wasn't it? Especially a goal that Professor Fitger—who probably knew a lot about being a writer—could help him attain.

In need of alone time when they got to Stonehenge, Fitger lagged behind the group, using his ankle, mostly healed, as an excuse. But Arva's voice was a bullhorn. In front of the Neolithic Houses, munchkin-like huts that mimicked the homes in which people had lived a few thousand years earlier, she informed the students that "the rooves are thatched. They are weaven from straw." The undergrads ignored her; they drank from their quart-sized water bottles or stared soullessly at their phones.

Fitger took a tube of antacids from his coat pocket—dinner the previous night had, once again, featured sausage—but found that its childproof lid might have defeated a safecracking team.

"Do you want me to open that for you?"

He looked up. There was *E for Eczema = Elwyn,* offering assistance. Fitger noticed the painful-looking cracked red rash on his hand.

Elwyn flushed. "Even my mom thinks it's gross," he said. "But it's not contagious. I'm supposed to use a cream, but I left it at home."

"I'd appreciate it. Thanks." Fitger gave him the antacids, and Elwyn prized off the lid.

In a voice that could have roused the dead from their coffins, Arva was explaining that the Neolithic period, or late Stone Age, was the "age of stone."

Fitger and Elwyn walked along the path, which was freckled with flat black circles of gum. Up ahead, the monoliths rose up from the ground with a preternatural, sentient power. Fitger chewed up a chalky white tablet and contemplated the time and dedication required to set a series of twenty-ton boulders upright in a ring. All those centuries of striving, and look what was left: a massive bluestone bracelet of unparsable symbols. "Elwyn, don't let me slow you down," he said. "Go ahead and join the rest of the group."

Elwyn brushed some dust from the sleeve of his coat. "I'd rather not." He stood aside and watched the other students posing for photos, Wyatt and Joe Ballo lifting Lin in their arms and holding her horizontally above the ground as if she were a crosspiece in a trilithon. "A lot of people find me annoying," he said. "I try not to be, but sometimes I think, well, so what? That's who I am."

"I understand what you mean—perhaps too well," Fitger said. "But it may not be the most profitable attitude." He stepped off the path to allow a group of primary school children, neatly uniformed and well-mannered, to walk chattering by. How absurdly young everyone was, he thought. Impossible, now, to imagine being his students' age, or vice versa: they hadn't reached the point in life at which various parts of their bodies—the precipitous headache, the stabbing pain (perhaps a blood clot?) in the groin—seemed to compete for the opportunity to foretell their demise. Fitger imagined the text of his obituary, a short, dull list of dates and facts accompanied by a memorial moment in the *Payne Daily Scribe:* "Professor and Department Chair Fades into Well-Deserved Oblivion."

The twins were sketching on two pads of paper, Wyatt was lying in the grass just off the path, and Brent was speaking softly to Sonia, perhaps confiding in her his plan to become a writer like Charles Dickens. The students took a few thousand photos, and soon it was time to walk back to the bus. Arva announced that their next stop would be Salisbury with its famous cathedral; the cathedral's chapter house, she said, held one of the four originals of the Magna Carta.

Lin yawned and stretched. She would tour the cathedral, she said, but she wasn't interested in the Magna Carta.

Arva startled. Did Fitger's students know about the Magna Carta? Did they know what it was?

"I hope you're not talking about me," Lin said. "I'm a government/pre-law major."

Arva said she was talking about everyone—but she was looking at Lin. "The Magna Carta is not just part of the British history, it is also the American."

They were approaching the parking lot. "Why is she talking to me like I'm an idiot?" Lin turned to Fitger. The Magna Carta was a fetishized document, created to codify the rule of a white male elite. "I don't need to look at it," she said, "because I live with that shit every day."

"You are ridiculous. And ignorant," Arva said. "I will ask you a question."

"I will ask *you* a question," Lin said. "Who the fuck do you think you are?"

Fitger stepped between them. "Let's try to—"

"No. We are finished trying," Arva said. Was Fitger going to let his student swear at her?

He pointed out that it was too late to stop her. "And," he said, "if she wants to close her eyes as we file past the Magna Carta, I—"

Arva erupted. Four Magna Cartas in existence, and one of them in Salisbury, she said, but Fitger hadn't bothered to prepare his students, he was lazy and they were lazy, he brought them to England but taught them nothing, they should all be ashamed. "It is their own history they refuse to care for. They want only to be clowns and to play."

Fitger turned for a final look at the monoliths and considered the idea of walking back up the path and standing silently forever among them. "Perhaps I should have deluged the group with meaningless monologues," he said. "But you've already taken that approach."

"You are an idiot man," Arva said. She snapped her fingers.

"We are done with our tour." She collected her things from the bus; she would make her way back to London on her own.

The students were supposed to have lunch before their viewing of the cathedral and the Magna Carta—Arva had made a reservation—but Arva was gone, and Fitger didn't remember the name of the restaurant or know where, in Salisbury, it was. So, like the leader of a troop of mendicants, he led the students down one street and up the next, peering into the windows of dining establishments, only to find them too expensive, too crowded, or, in the words of one of the twins, "bottom line: gross."

"I'm glad you got rid of her," Lin said. "I mean, of Arva. She was pissing me off. I've never seen anyone get fired. Do you think she'll sue for wrongful termination?"

"I didn't fire her," Fitger said, wondering, as they turned a corner, whether they had passed that corner a few minutes before. He paused and watched Wyatt, who had a habit of lagging behind and nearly getting struck by cars, dropping some money into a busker's cup.

They walked past a pub, but it held only three small tables, all full of inebriates.

Brent caught up with Fitger at the front of the group and suggested, not for the first time, that they look for Italian food or for pizza. "Something that, like, *tastes* good," he said. He was tired of eating English food.

Elwyn, behind them, pointed out that Brent had just used the word "like." During a moment of grammatical pique a few days before, Fitger had forbidden them, unless expressing a preference or comparing one thing to another, to make use of that word.

Sonia said she didn't want pizza; it had too many carbs. One of the twins suggested Thai. What about the place they had passed twenty minutes ago, the one with the awning? Felicity anxiously confided that she didn't have money with her; she might have accidentally left her wallet behind on the bus.

A horn sounded off, to Fitger's left, signaling another near–traffic death for Wyatt. Fitger paused by a mailbox and tried to call up a map of Salisbury on his phone, but it sent him directions to a town in Australia. If they ever reached the cathedral, he thought, he would fall to his knees and ask to begin his working life over in a different profession.

Up ahead, some of the undergrads had discovered a bakery, and Joe Ballo was holding the door while they filed in. The bakery window held a selection of biscuits, pies, jelly rolls, eclairs, tarts, petit fours, and a smiling oversized cardboard cutout of the queen.

Lin pointed out that Felicity didn't have money and the students had been told that lunch would be paid for, so Fitger took out his wallet and passed out some bills. He held one out to Xanna.

"Thanks, but I don't need anything," she said. "I'm not really feeling the rest of the trip today, so I'm going to head on back to the bus."

Fitger told her that she would feel better after a snack— and they would probably reach the cathedral (he had only a dim idea of where it might be) after another ten-minute walk.

"I'm tired of walking, though," Xanna said. Besides: Lin

122

would be boycotting the Magna Carta, and Joe Ballo would clearly not be climbing the three hundred claustrophobic steps of the Salisbury spire.

"Joe has a good reason to avoid the spire," Fitger said. Were there really three hundred steps? "And you're not the only person here who's feeling tired. We're all tired. Believe me, I'm tired."

Xanna stepped off the sidewalk to make room for a woman who was pushing a stroller. "Maybe you should go back to the bus, too." She smiled.

"No one is going back to the bus." Fitger reminded Xanna that part of her grade depended on her full engagement with the group. "Do you have a topic for your final essay?"

She ran a hand through a tuft of her hair. "Yeah. I already told you: I want to write about the London Eye. I went on it again yesterday, and it—"

"Do you have a thesis?"

She tilted her head. "I didn't hear you grilling anyone else about their thesis. Anyway, I started writing, and I know what you look for in an essay. Besides, I don't stress about grades. I had an A minus in your class last year."

Fitger blinked. "You were in my class last year?"

"Yeah. Contemporary Fiction. I sat in the back. There was a guy in the front row who raised his hand all the time and disagreed with everything you said."

Fitger remembered—it was impossible to forget—the disputatious student in the front row; but, skimming through that previous year's class in his mind, he failed to situate Xanna's image. "I thought you looked familiar," he said. "But . . ."

"You probably forgot me because I didn't finish the class," Xanna said. "Plus, I changed my last name over the summer after my parents got divorced. My dad's been a prick so I took my mom's last name—Blythe. And I used to go by Roxanne. That's my original first name, but I'm Xanna now. So I went from Roxanne Reynolds to Xanna Blythe."

"I remember now," Fitger said. "You usually came in a few minutes late. And you didn't have—" He gestured toward her rusty blue hair.

She nodded. "I shaved my head last year. It was a phase."

Felicity emerged from the bakery with a trio of candy-coated pretzels. Did she owe Fitger money? Did he want a pretzel?

Fitger declined.

"Anyway," Xanna said, "I'm off to the bus. My mom wants to FaceTime."

"Wait a minute." Fitger stopped her. "You were on the London Eye yesterday?"

"Yeah. I'm kind of obsessed with it," Xanna said. "I don't know if I can pull it off, but I want to write about the feeling that, when you look down from your little capsule—"

"You were supposed to be at the John Soane museum yesterday," he said. "You told me you weren't feeling well."

"That was in the morning." She shrugged. "I felt better in the afternoon."

The twins came toward them, each of them holding a chocolate eclair.

"I want you to make up the work from this trip that you've missed," Fitger said. "Every bit of it."

Xanna took a bite of one of the twins' eclairs. "I don't get it," she said, licking cream from her finger. "Why are you pissed at me all of a sudden?"

Fitger told her that he wasn't "pissed." But she could Face-Time with her mother later. "Right now, tired or not, you'll stay with the group."

"What is this, the army? Are you telling me I can't take a break if I need one?"

"A break? That's what you need?" Fitger's voice was getting louder. "You need a *break*?" A little holiday away from the group? Some peace and quiet?" Xanna took a step back, and a barely discernible voice in Fitger's head reminded him that he was a professor, and Xanna his student. He struggled to modulate his tone. "I don't like to see you making excuses," he said. "You don't do yourself any favors when you indulge in the idea of being sick."

Brent emerged from the bakery carrying what looked like a three-layer cake. "I got a bunch of forks for this monster," he said.

"Wow. I don't believe this." Xanna shook her head. "I'm not making excuses. Are you accusing me of being a fake?"

"I'm not accusing you of anything," Fitger said. "I'm just saying that—Brent, move away from me with that thing."

"You said I 'indulge' in the idea of being sick," Xanna said.

Brent held out a fork. "Here. At least try the frosting. It's buttercream."

"I'm not sticking around for this," Xanna said. "I'll be on the bus."

"What's she so cranky about?" Lin asked.

Fitger pierced the cake with a fork. He watched Xanna jog through a group of tourists, the cobalt flame of her hair swallowed up by the crowd. He had never shouted at a student before. He'd apologize later. Right now, there was nothing else to do but continue their tour.

EIGHT

"Didn't you read their health disclosures?" Janet asked. "Lupus: it must have been listed on her application."

"I read those applications a month ago and forgot all about them." It was 2:00 a.m. in London, and Fitger was sitting up in bed, having spent several insomniac hours in self-reproach and recrimination. Xanna's five-hundred-word essay (like her others, odd but well written) consisted of a guide to her disease, including its symptoms—intermittent pain, fatigue, fever, hair loss, sensitivity to light, and a potentially short-ened life span—all of which were exacerbated by the "added stress of skepticism from family and friends." In a postscript, she said that, since Fitger seemed to want to punish her for her choice of topic on the final assignment, she no longer intended to write about the subject she preferred: the London Eye.

"I assume you apologized?" Janet asked.

"Profusely. I abased myself. But she isn't speaking to me—which is understandable." He looked up at the California-shaped stain on his bedroom ceiling, which had extended its borders into parts of Oregon and Nevada. A drip had begun to form near Sacramento. "Nine more days in this miserable country," he said.

Janet suggested that it might not be fair to blame his wretchedness on the U.K. "Maybe you can shift more responsibility onto your Danish/Albanian friend."

"That would be a *no*," Fitger said. "We had a little disagreement about the Magna Carta, apparently a sore point with Romanians. If I had known that—"

"Hang on," Janet said. "I left the water running in the tub."

Fitger climbed out of bed and studied his ceiling. It was definitely dripping. He found a plastic basin under the bathroom sink and set it on the floor, nudging it into the appropriate place with his foot.

"All right. Ready," Janet said. "I didn't realize you got all hot and bothered about the Magna Carta."

"Yes, it's just one more thing you wish you'd known about me," Fitger said. He heard the squeal of faucets being tightened. Janet had a special fondness, in winter, for a steaming hot bath. He remembered sitting on the closed lid of the toilet and arguing with her about a story—which he had just read aloud—by Ivan Turgenev; when she was tired of arguing with him, she pulled the shower curtain closed between them, as if shutting an audience away from the stage at the end of a play. "In case you were going to ask me about it, I'm working on your recommendation letter," he said. "I meant to have it finished by now, but I—"

She cut him off. "I don't want you to worry about that letter anymore. You have enough going on."

A drip fell from the vicinity of Santa Rosa. "Are you getting into the tub now?" he asked.

A sharp intake of breath and a subtle splash served as his answer. The fact that his ex-wife was willing to talk to him during her sacred soaking time felt portentous. "Why are you telling me not to worry about the recommendation?"

"Oh . . . because." Janet sighed—the sigh of a tub-loving person immersed in hot water. "You were clearly struggling to write it. Now you're free of the task."

Fitger glanced at the recycling bin next to his desk, full of discarded drafts of the letter, torn in half. "You found someone else to write it for you," he said.

No answer from Janet.

"Who?"

"Don't worry about it, Jay. You're off the hook."

"But you already sent me the link. It won't look good if I don't submit a recommendation. I can aim for tomorrow."

Janet said she would prefer that he drop it.

"But I'd like to do it. I insist."

"And I insist that you *not* do it." Her voice had entered the dangerous register Fitger privately referred to as the key of E-flat.

He heard the squeak of a faucet. She was topping up the hot water; she always used her left foot to do this—she had very strong and dexterous toes. "If your new letter-writer is Thor," he said, as another drip landed in the basin behind him, "you might want to consider the fact that he hasn't taught or worked at Payne for more than ten years."

"That's correct. He's at Oxford. Maybe you've heard of it," Janet said.

Fitger asked her if she had read Thor's writing; his prose style bespoke a fondness for blowsy and flavorless sentences.

Furthermore, did Janet want her future boss to find fault with her file because of missing or substandard references?

"I'll provide an excuse for you," Janet said. "I'll mention your two broken arms."

Fitger wondered if she was engaged in some wishful thinking. He listened for bathing sounds—washrag, soap, loofah—but heard nothing. Janet had reached the peak bath experience. This was the point at which he used to read to her: hearing the rusted shriek of the faucet, he would enter the bathroom and find her leaning back in the tub against her favorite inflatable cushion, eyes closed, the water lapping at her neck as if at a shoreline. Should he offer to read to her now? He looked around the apartment for something that would pique her interest and came upon Wyatt's account of his visit to a tanning salon: I should of exfoliated first, I have big red bumps now on my back and all over my ass.

There had to be something more uplifting. Ah, here was the appropriately titled *Bath: A Guide*, which Herman Trout, learning about the altercation with Arva, had shoved under Fitger's door. He turned to the "Quick Facts" page, which informed him that the city and its charms lay only two and a half hours by bus from London. Two and a half hours! Unendurable, he thought. Skimming a few paragraphs, he was given to understand that he would have a chance to sip sulfuric waters and learn about Bath buns and bricks and invalid chairs. "It's no wonder you and I had the sense not to go there," he muttered. "What the hell is a Bath bun?"

He heard only silence on the other end.

"Hello? Janet? Hello, are you there?"

JOSEPH BALLO, JANUARY 22 ASSIGNMENT

Professor, I am writing this essay about our trip to Stone Henge as a compare-and-contrast. I am not sure if it works that way (you will let me know.)

The compare-and-contrast aspect is that I want to talk about two different places, one is the church I attended before my time in foster care the other is Stone Henge and its circle of stones. Both are Places of Mystery which I have explained before is one of my interests. The church I attended was called the Redeemer of the Constant Flame. It was not a warm or welcoming place. When I asked my uncle who I was living with at that time why we didn't have music at that church he said God doesn't care if you can play the guitar.

"Looks like a leak," the Trout said. He was perched on a ladder in Fitger's bedroom, prodding the stain on the ceiling with his knuckly fingers. "Definitely a leak."

Fitger put his students' essays aside; he took off his glasses and attempted to wipe them clean on his shirt. "I suppose that's the usual term for water dripping from the ceiling," he said. "How long will it take to fix?"

The Trout jabbed at the stain above his head. "Remains to be seen. Could be a pipe. Could be something else." Bits of plaster were trickling onto the floor.

One of the twins knocked at the door, which the Trout had propped open; she was dropping off her most recent coauthored assignment, made of what appeared to be dozens of crushed aluminum cans. "Hey, Herm." She waved. "What are you doing up there?"

The Trout hitched up his pants. "He's got a problem with his ceiling."

Fitger accepted the aluminum can sculpture without comment and said that he didn't consider the ceiling or the problem *his*.

"Cool," the twin said. She told Fitger that her sibling would email the text that went with the cans. "Poker at seven, Herm?" she asked.

The Trout gave a thumbs-up.

Fitger waited until the twin was gone. "You're playing poker with my students?"

"Thursdays," the Trout said.

Fitger had no desire to play poker with his undergrads, but he wondered what sort of sums were changing hands. Debris continued dribbling down from the ceiling. "Do you think a drop cloth would be a good idea?"

"Shouldn't need one," the Trout said. He directed Fitger's attention to what had become a sizable hole in the plaster. The tricky thing about a leak, he explained, was that even a small one like this could lead to mold. Or, worse: fungus. Mold was one thing, but you didn't want to have to deal with fungus. That was nasty stuff. Even breathing its fumes could be a problem.

"*Is there* fungus?" Fitger asked.

The Trout shrugged.

For the next two days, Fitger read his students' assignments in the lobby downstairs.

ELWYN P. YANG

OPTIONAL/STUDENT'S CHOICE ASSIGNMENT:
THE KIT-CAT-CAFÉ

At the Kit-Cat-Café, cats are not allowed near where the food is prepared so the café area was free of hair and very clean. Because of my allergies I have never had a cat but an afternoon spent among them, if I am not picking them up or holding them near my face, was probably fine. There were seven cats on the premises. Three were black-and-white, one was all white, one all black, and the others—

"A cat café." Fitger scratched his head. "You visited a restaurant full of cats."

"Yeah." Elwyn sat across the table from Fitger, his head hanging forward on his neck as if dangling loosely from a hinge. "The cats weren't allowed in the restaurant part. They had to stay on their side."

"Right," Fitger said. "That makes sense. It's just . . . surprising. I didn't realize that you were interested in cats. And I thought you were planning a graveyard tour."

"I was." Elwyn had worn Fitger down and received permission to write about Highgate Cemetery: he had been particularly looking forward to Egyptian Avenue, with its row of mausoleum doors and even doorbells—a promenade of posh apartments for the dead. "But Felicity invited me to the cat café. She didn't want to go by herself."

133

Fitger contemplated the essay. A group of cats is called a clowder. The male is a tom, the female a molly or a queen. A separate section on the following page, devoted to a breed of cat with smaller ears, was introduced with a subhead: The Scottish Fold.

"You said you wanted me to branch out." Elwyn chewed at his lip. "You said you wanted me to experiment with other topics."

"Yes, that's true. A range of subjects is—"

"Hi, Elwyn!"

Elwyn's head spun so abruptly Fitger thought he might have injured his neck. Here was Felicity coming toward them. She was going out for a while. She needed some more colored markers—and some of those little sticky notes in different shapes. She used to have heart-shaped sticky notes, but she didn't know if she would find those here. Did Elwyn want to come with her? Or was he meeting with Professor Fitger?

"No. He's just talking to me." Elwyn stood, gesturing vaguely in Fitger's direction.

Fitger confirmed that he had been saying nothing of any importance, and Felicity and Elwyn went off in search of supplies.

Though the upcoming visit to Bath was the final daylong trip of their three-week term, by definition leading to the denouement of his time in London, Fitger had been looking toward it with dread. Xanna was still not speaking to him because of the way he had "made fun of her illness" at Stonehenge (proving to one and all that he was a callous human being and sadistic instructor); furthermore, in Arva's absence, he would need to serve as docent, though he'd scarcely glanced at the introduction to *Bath: A Guide.* The students seemed equally unenthusiastic about a third bus trip to a famous attraction. A collective malaise had infected the group.

The evening before their departure, wondering if he might bribe the driver of the minibus to release the air from a few of his tires, Fitger heard a banging sound coming from the lobby below. He waited to see if the Trout would take care of it, but the banging continued. It was almost midnight. Perhaps the Trout was being fleeced of his savings by one of the twins, during a game of six-card stud.

Holding the handrail in case of errant tools on the steps, he went downstairs. In the alcove he found Brent, heavily sweating during an assault on a vending machine.

"I put my change in, but it tells me I didn't," Brent said. "It's the second time this thing's ripped me off."

There was nothing in any of the vending machines that, in Fitger's opinion, anyone other than a person near starvation would be willing to eat, but he dug a handful of coins from his pocket.

Brent had a handful of coins of his own, and they compared their collections. What inspired the British to manufacture so many different denominations of coins? Brent sighed and inserted what appeared to Fitger a random accumulation, and they thunked into the gullet of the machine with a satisfied sound. Brent's finger hovered over E7, a cellophane-wrapped cupcake with a worrisome yellow stripe across its facade.

"You haven't turned in your last two assignments, Brent," Fitger said.

"Yeah." Studying the offerings in front of him, Brent tipped his head to the side as if emptying water from a ewer. "I don't know if I can get those done."

"Why's that?" Fitger tried to keep his tone curious instead of judgmental.

After a moment of indecision, Brent chose B1: a hideous hamburgeresque option that landed in the tray below with a dispiriting thump. "I don't know. I haven't been wanting to write very much in the last few days. I was thinking maybe I could get an exemption."

"An extension?" Fitger asked. Somewhere on the syllabus, he had specified NO EXTENSIONS OR INCOMPLETES EXCEPT BY PROFESSOR APPROVAL IN CASES OF EMERGENCY, but whatever fortitude he had felt at the beginning of the trip had turned to ennui.

Brent had unwrapped B1 and managed to fit most of it into his mouth; he spoke through the filling. He needed to take a break from writing for a while, he said. He thought it would be best if he turned in the rest of his assignments, or maybe some of them, the ones he could finish, when they got back to Payne.

"But you'll be enrolled in other classes by then. You'll be much busier." Though he wasn't hungry, Fitger found his attention being drawn to one of the vending machine options: C4, a rectangular package of crackers and cheese.

"I'm thinking I might take next semester off," Brent said. "But I'd stay on campus, you know? Maybe sleep on somebody's floor or at the gym, but not go to school."

"I think that's called 'trespassing,'" Fitger said. "Why would you take a semester off?"

Brent leaned heavily against the wall and looked down at his shoes. "I don't know if the college diploma thing is for me," he said. "Other people like school a lot more than I do. I went to Payne because Sonia was going. I just want to stick around until she graduates."

Fitger mentally added a charge of *stalking* to *trespassing*. "I don't think that's a good idea, Brent. Maybe you came to college because Sonia did, but you're here of your own accord now. Even if you're both exploring different relationships and moving in different directions, you—"

Brent cut him off. "What do you mean, we're *both* exploring?"

"What?" Fitger purchased the crackers.

"You said me and Sonia are both exploring different relationships. Did she say something to you?"

Retrieving his selection from the vending machine, Fitger reminded Brent of his reputedly ironclad policy regarding discussion of the personal or romantic lives of his students.

"Huh. Okay." Brent threw his trash into the bin. "We're not really broken up," he said. "Sometimes she wants me to leave her alone, you know, so I do, but we're still hanging out. She just wants to think about stuff, you know? To take time. Like she wants to think about what things are going to be like when we get back to Payne. I don't think she would cheat the way I did. I think she still loves me." He leaned against the wall, arms folded across his chest; his face wore an expression of hopeful belligerence.

No matter what happened in regard to his relationship,

Fitger said, Brent was young and he was strong. He had many years ahead of him; with or without Sonia, he would be all right.

Brent blinked, as if a cinder had blown into his eye. "Maybe what happened with you was different. Maybe you didn't have things in common, and that's why you and your wife got divorced."

"Brent, I'm not going to—"

"So I don't think you should give me advice," Brent said. He asked Fitger if he was going to eat his crackers.

"Here." Fitger handed them over. "I don't want you to drop out. I thought you were planning to be a writer like Charles Dickens."

Brent sighed and opened the crackers. If he didn't drop out, he said, maybe he could do an independent project with Fitger. Maybe they could write something together under both of their names and get it published. Brent would give the idea some thought, and he would let Fitger know when they got back to Payne.

An hour later, finally getting into bed (the ceiling above him was unevenly patched), Fitger saw his phone light up with a message: *Job offer*, it said. Janet.

He propped himself up with a pillow against the headboard and texted her back. He hadn't submitted her recommendation; wasn't the deadline next week?

The day before yesterday, Janet wrote. *But it doesn't matter because I got the offer. And they were thrilled to get a letter from Thor.*

Of course they were, Fitger thought. The world loves an

idiot. His pillow slid from behind him, disappearing into the gap between headboard and wall. He struggled to reach it. *Have you accepted yet?*

Debating salary.

In any debate, Fitger's ex was tenacious. *So your clown of a dean will have to open his wallet for you,* he said. Janet's boss, the dean of the law school, had an interest in circus and could occasionally be seen riding a unicycle around the Payne campus.

Janet responded with a question mark. What did the dean have to do with it?

Still attempting to retrieve his pillow, Fitger thrust his hand between headboard and box spring, fingers spidering around the bed's metal frame. The fleshy pad of his thumb met something sharp: probably a shiv, he thought, abandoned by a previous inmate. Damn: there was a gash in his skin, a zigzag wound that seemed to hesitate for a few seconds before welling with blood. *Haven cut my s self,* he typed. Would he need a tetanus shot? Stitches? He cradled the hand on his way to the bathroom and ran it under cold water. Blood swirled clockwise down the drain.

You OK? Janet asked.

Yes. He was fine—as long as lockjaw didn't set in. His hand was throbbing now. He wrapped it up in a towel. Wasn't her offer at the law school?

No.

He put the phone down and ransacked the bureau for his medical kit: a plastic bag containing a jumble of antibiotic cream, aspirin, gauze, tape, and—for purposes of distraction—a battered package of M&M's. He opened the M&M's

and ate some, then squirted a ribbon of soap onto his hand and held it under the faucet again. The cut looked bad—jagged and floppy, like the mouth of a fish. He managed to cut a few lengths of gauze with a scissors while drops of blood spattered the floor. *Where is it?* he asked.

Chicago, Janet answered. *Fill you in later. On my way out to dinner.*

Someone was knocking at the door of Fitger's apartment. A knock after midnight meant an emergency of some kind: traffic accident, venereal disease, assault, beheading . . . "One minute," he yelled. He texted Janet: Did she mean Chicago in Illinois?

Of course Illinois. Bye. Running late.

Fitger bandaged his hand with the gauze and texted her back. What time would she be home from her dinner? *You didn't tell me you were applying to jobs out of state.*

You didn't ask.

The knocking continued.

I'll call in an hour, he wrote. *We'll talk then.*

I'll be out late.

"Professor Fitger? Are you there?"

"Fuck." Fitger tossed his phone onto the bed and answered the door.

The good news: Wyatt was alive and at least intermittently awake, though he did smell strongly of vomit and booze. Fitger was able to get him to swallow a piece of bread and prop him upright, with a large paper bag on the floor near his feet. Joe Ballo and Lin had dropped him off, having decided that someone in authority should oversee his condition. Fitger soon realized that he was alone, in his pajamas, with an inebriated undergrad in the middle of the night. He quickly got dressed in the bedroom, propped the door to his apartment open, and turned on the lights. Wyatt squinted and moaned in his sleep. On the couch beside him—they had probably fallen out of his pocket—were several crumpled pieces of paper. Fitger rescued them, smoothing them out.

A CONVERSATION WITH A STRANGER IN ENGLAND

(This is my paper from last week, sorry I forgot to hand it in, I found it under some other stuff in my room)

BY WYATT FRANKLIN

The stranger I met and talked to was an old woman one night at the Five Swans. Inside the Swans it is always dark, with a floor that is sticky under your feet and furniture that might belong to your grandmother if she was a person who went blind in her old age and never wiped up her spills.

The woman was sitting at the bar, she past me a dish of peanuts and asked who I was and where I was from. Her coat was unsnapped and I could see that she wore a small dog in a front-pack, the way a mother would carry a human baby on her chest.

Helen (her name) was at least sixty, with huge deep wrinkles in her face like river beds in a dry part of the country that has run out of water. (I know you have told me to cut back on my metaphors but I have always been told it is a more interesting way to write, to have colorful speech.) Her long gray hair was fassened with pins at the top of her head. She gave Pete (that was her dog, I think part Chihuahua) some peanuts to chew on. I said I had never seen a dog eat nuts, I thought they were allergic and she said he ate whatever he liked. Her mouth opened and closed like she was chewing for him. Pete chewed and chewed on that little nut. They looked like two puppets with their chins going up and down.

I should have gone home I had enough by then but I ordered

another Tennent's at the bar. I don't usually talk to women who are Helen's age but we had this assignment so when the rest of my group left I stayed behind. My memory is not as good when I drink so I don't know how the conversation went or how it happened but I told Helen about my friend Low who died last year and all the sudden she was shouting, she was grabbing my hands with her swollen hands, her fingers clutching me like the roots of old trees tangled in soil and she was telling me that I should have been with him, which is something I've thought about a lot, we were supposed to hang out that night, me and Lowell, but when Jack wanted to come I ditched, I lied to Low and said I had plans.

Pete was staring at me with his round black eyes that were round like marbles and I thought maybe Helen was a homeless or mentally impaired person, because her clothes weren't very clean but still the things she was saying, it is hard for me to repeat them exactly, were hitting me hard.

That was my conversation with a stranger, I tried to cut out the stuff that doesn't matter concentrating like you said on the ones that rise to the top of my head like cream. The part I will think about most is Helen's hands twisting in mine when she said I shouldn't have lied to my friend and ditched him, her dog Pete tipping toward me like a little baby from his place on her chest.

If the point of this assignment is to tell about a conversation that we will remember then this is the one. Because I think Helen was right what she said about me and it is a hard feeling that comes to me sometimes when I ask myself if I have already failed at the things in life that matter most, and I will never be what I was supposed to become.

It was after 3:00 a.m. in London when Janet finally answered the texts—about half a dozen—that Fitger had sent while watching Wyatt twitch in his sleep. The job she'd been offered wasn't terribly different from the work she did at Payne, she explained, but the university in Chicago was better. She still hadn't shared the news with anyone in her office because she didn't want to sign on the dotted line until a decision was made about salary, but most people probably suspected that she was up for a change. She asked why Fitger was awake at 3:20 a.m.

Drunken student in my room. Didn't she think she should have told him that she was applying for a position outside of Payne?

No, she said. *Why is there a drunken student in your room?*

He didn't bother to answer. *You should have been honest with me. You owed me that much.*

Janet said she didn't owe him anything. Thor had offered his congratulations.

Well, of course he had offered them, Fitger thought. And he had probably reissued his invitation to a bacchanal at his Italian villa. Janet would be packing her suitcase soon. Fitger pictured his flight crossing paths with hers above Greenland, and the dog, Rogaine, waiting at home for him, gnawing the leg of a favorite chair.

Wyatt had slumped toward the arm of the couch; Fitger propped him back up and texted Janet again. It made no sense for her to move to Chicago. She was probably half a dozen years from retirement, and her entire life was built around Payne. What about her university book club and her yoga class and her tennis group, not to mention the odd-looking women with whom, on Wednesdays, he often saw her power walking at lunchtime along the paths of the south campus? Her house—within walking distance of her office—was nearly paid off, for god's sake.

You used to tell me you loved Chicago, she wrote.

Well, yes, in the abstract, he had loved Chicago. Like most of the faculty at Payne, he would, at one point in time, have sacrificed a functioning limb for the chance to be hired away from the humdrum backwater in which they worked. But that was years ago now, and he had given up on the idea of being wooed by any other institution and assumed that Janet had made her peace with Payne as well. *You asked for a letter but you weren't honest with me,* he wrote. *You should have been honest.*

You never wrote the letter! she answered. *And maybe I didn't tell you where I was applying because I was afraid you would have sabotaged me.*

Fitger stared at his phone. *Uncalled for,* he wrote.

You're not denying it.

Do you deny being manipulative and deceitful?

I'm turning my phone off, Janet wrote.

Fitger began another text but before he could send it, she texted again: *The only reason I mentioned the job to you at all was because of the dog.*

At 6:00 a.m. Fitger made two cups of coffee, deliberately clattering the rusted kettle on the two-burner stove. Wyatt sat up. He rubbed his eyes with the heels of his hands—the gesture, Fitger thought, of a very small boy. "Did I stay here all night?"

Fitger handed him a mug and asked him how he was feeling.

"Lousy."

"That makes two of us." Fitger had spent most of the night awake and upright in a wooden chair. He would need a chiropractic appointment, he thought, if he ever hoped to stand entirely erect again. "You should probably eat something," he said. "Toast or a sandwich. I may have some of those English biscuits."

"I didn't think I drank that much," Wyatt said. "I mean, not at first. It won't happen again."

Fitger rummaged through the cabinets and found a sleeve of digestive biscuits, which he set in their wrapper on the arm of the couch. "I get the impression that it happens a lot."

Wyatt acknowledged that it happened more often than it probably should. "But I guess it's too late to send me home."

Oh, that there were a way to misbehave and be sent home, Fitger thought. He knew that somewhere, among thickets of paper still in his suitcase, there was a form signed by Wyatt on which he had promised, during the twenty-two days of the trip, to abstain from use or overindulgence in legal or illegal substances and to remember that he was a representative of Payne University, which—although no one outside a hundred-mile radius had ever heard of it—supposedly had a sterling reputation to uphold. With only three days left of the trip, it might not make sense to send him home, but there were other sanctions. Should Fitger report him, he could be suspended when he got back to Payne—or even expelled.

He went into the bedroom and returned with a travel-size bottle of aspirin from his medical kit. He shook three round

146

pills into his hand, keeping one for himself and offering the others to Wyatt. Then he slipped the bottle into the pocket of his shirt. "I read your essay," he said. "The 'Conversation with a Stranger.' About that woman at the Five Swans."

Wyatt swallowed the aspirin and winced as he sipped the coffee. "What happened to your hand?" he asked.

Fitger had rebandaged his injury during the night; blood was visible here and there through the gauze. "It's nothing. Just a cut. Listen, Wyatt. That woman in the pub doesn't know you. And from the way you describe her, it sounds like she wasn't in her right mind."

"It must have been a bad cut," Wyatt said. "There's blood on your floor over there. That's the second time you got hurt since we've been in England."

Fitger nodded; he would be lucky to get home without drowning upright in the shower or being set upon by a wild boar. "Wyatt, I don't want you to let a total stranger in a bar—"

"Did that happen last night? Because of me?" Wyatt was staring as if bewitched at Fitger's hand. "I mean, did you cut yourself when you carried me in?"

Fitger explained that Lin and Joe Ballo had been the ones to carry him. "The cut on my hand happened before you arrived."

Wyatt nodded and reached for the biscuits. Fitger was trying to decide how to phrase what he wanted to tell him: *Your friend is dead but you are still here.*

Through the window, the clouds were thinning, the sky streaked with pale light.

"Sorry about my essay being late," Wyatt said. "I lost it for a while. But I guess it was folded up in my pocket. You already read it?"

Fitger handed over the essay. He had given it a B-minus. "You tend to overwork your descriptions," he said. "But that business of the dog eating peanuts, and the two chins going up and down—that was well done."

"Thanks." Wyatt gestured toward Fitger's bandaged hand. "It looks like you wrapped it up pretty well. I could have helped you if I wasn't out of it. Did you know I'm a Wilderness First Responder?"

"Yes, I seem to remember that," Fitger said. "Wyatt—"

"I took a whole course," Wyatt said. "I even got credit. So I could have bandaged that for you."

Fitger rubbed his uninjured hand over his face. He had completely lost track of what he wanted to say. "Wyatt, this cut on my hand was not an emergency."

"We did dislocations, frostbite, fractures . . . We were ten days in the middle of nowhere in Colorado," Wyatt said. "But I haven't used much of it since—all the stuff that I learned. Which sucks, you know? Because taking the course made me feel useful. Like I could do something useful to help. Like I was prepared."

"My hand is fine," Fitger said.

"Right. But if I had been here," Wyatt said, "maybe I could have helped."

NINE

During the bus ride to Bath, Fitger stared at the back of the driver's head with its horizontal folds of skin and considered Janet's last text before she turned off—or claimed to have turned off—her phone: *The only reason I mentioned the job to you at all was because of the dog.* She was giving him notice: She was planning to move to Chicago and take Rogaine with her. She had asked for a letter of recommendation not because she needed one from him, but so that she could tell him, later, that he should have known she would take the dog; she had informed him of her intention when letting him know that she was applying for jobs.

Leaning forward, he asked the driver how much longer until they reached Bath.

"An hour and a half" was the answer.

Fitger sat back in his seat: even in the dentist's chair, he thought, time never passed at such a crawl. Ignoring a student fracas behind him (a debate about death by earthquake vs. volcano), he took his phone out of his pocket and reread Janet's texts. She didn't say when the new job would start, or when she would move. Astonishing, he thought, that they had been divorced for ten years, a decade that inspired in him the desire to live vast swaths of his life over, this time while paying attention. Toward the rear of the bus, the students continued their desultory quarrel. Fitger checked the time on his phone: an hour and twenty more minutes. Beneath the digital numbers, he saw his screen-saver picture of Rogaine. It wasn't a flattering likeness, as the dog was gnawing on a bone with a snarling, covetous gleam in his eye, but it was an image that Fitger enjoyed, in part because Janet always claimed that it made the dog look possessed.

Soon after their arrival in Bath, a rare stroke of luck: Fitger connected their group with a free two-hour walking tour, which was conducted by a heavily whiskered man who addressed most of his remarks to his luxuriant beard. Along with a family of Italians, who chattered among themselves and listened to nothing the tour guide said, they strolled along the Royal Crescent and through Victoria Park and the Circus, and heard something woolly and indistinct about the 1942 Baedeker Blitz. When they passed the Jane Austen Centre, Brent paused to ask a woman in Regency dress for her opinion on the NBA All-Star teams.

The two hours concluded at Pulteney Bridge, their guide wishing them a *something-something-something* during the rest of their stay. Sonia asked if, instead of lunch, they could have a high tea. The twins wanted to go to the Holburne Museum. Elwyn had a ghost walk in mind, and Felicity was hoping to shop for souvenirs.

Fitger announced that the afternoon plan was for each student to do exactly what they wanted, independent of the instructor. He was leaving them to their own devices until 4:00 p.m., when he would meet them at the Roman Baths for their afternoon tour. He watched them disperse. When all were thoroughly out of range, he found a small colorless café, where he ordered a salad and a cinnamon scone and tea. He checked his phone for any updates from Janet about her job or the dog, but she had sent nothing. It probably made sense, he supposed, for the dog to go with her. She was the one who cooked Rogaine homemade meals and allowed him to sleep on his own dog-sized tuffet at the foot of her bed. When he stayed at Fitger's, Rogaine slept in the closet, inhaling the scent of a plastic bin full of soiled clothes.

Lunch was soon set before him. Fitger's salad—why could the British not make salad?—exhibited symptoms of prolonged refrigeration: two pale slabs of tomato and two thin leaves of iceberg lettuce flanked a dollop of mayonnaise. He nudged the mayo aside. On the other hand, he thought, Janet shouldn't *assume* that she could take the dog with her. It was something they'd have to discuss. It was true that adopting Rogaine had been her idea (Fitger had been skeptical, because he'd never had a dog, and he and Janet were already divorced) and also true that she had pressed him to sign as co-owner. Sharing a pet would mean less work for each of them, she had pointed out, and the dog could be walked back and forth between their two homes. In Fitger's case, she couldn't help saying, this would offer an opportunity for some much-needed exercise and time out of doors.

Fitger ate a slice of the pale tomato. He remembered the process of the dog's adoption, which required a background check that most NASA employees probably wouldn't have passed. He remembered signing the official papers, which specified that Jason Fitger and Janet Matthias would share responsibility and expenses for the hound/lab/beagle/shepherd mix being released, after almost a year at various shelters because of poor behavior, into their care. He bit into the cinnamon scone, which crumbled in his mouth like gypsum. It was also true that Janet oversaw the dog's grooming and maintenance; but hadn't she insisted that it was Fitger's turn, when he got back, to take the dog to the vet? And hadn't he, only a week or two before he left, extracted—at great risk to himself—a sizable thistle from the animal's paw?

Here was the crux of the problem: Janet hadn't been honest in her intentions. Her plan all along had been to move and take the dog. It was underhanded. Treacherous. And she had accused *him* of wanting to undermine *her*!

He paid for his food, leaving half of it on his plate, and followed a hand-holding couple out of the café. If Janet actually thought that he would sabotage her attempt to get a new job, why did she ask him for a recommendation? He walked through Queen Square. Here was the Jane Austen Centre again, but the woman in Regency dress had been replaced by a man in a frock coat. Feeling restless, Fitger checked the time on his phone and saw the screen-saver picture of Rogaine. He paused on the sidewalk and looked at it—at the sinister curl in the upper lip and the malevolent gleam in the eyes. He sent Janet a text: *You can't have the dog.*

The students—all but D.B., who had recently sent greetings to the group from Budapest—were waiting for him when he arrived at four o'clock at the Roman Baths. Here was success: the students had survived their assorted individual adventures and regrouped as instructed, without a guide. Lin was organizing a thumb-wrestling competition. Did Fitger want to participate? No? She glanced at his bandaged right hand. He could play lefty. Did he want them to think he was a boring person?

"Yes, very much so," he said.

They entered the Victorian reception hall with its white domed ceiling. Felicity, next to Fitger while they waited in line for the audio guides, showed him the souvenirs she had purchased: an I LOVE BATH keychain, a Bath tea towel, and a feline raincoat with a Union Jack pattern for her cat, Mrs. Gray. Sonia was applying a new shade of lipstick; one of the twins was getting a sketchbook out of her bag.

Fitger's phone rang as he was trailing behind the students on their way to the famous terrace, with its quadrangle of statues overlooking the water.

"I hoped you wouldn't be a pain in the ass about this," Janet said.

"I'm at the Roman Baths," Fitger answered. "With the students. It's not a good time to talk."

"Fine. Let me just quickly say that if I take the job, the dog will go with me."

Fitger watched the undergrads taking photos of themselves and each other—but mostly themselves. "You said 'if,' " he told Janet. "Not 'when' but 'if' you take the job."

"*If and when,*" Janet said. "I'm talking to some realtors in Chicago tomorrow and looking into renting out my house for a year."

"The word 'renting' has a temporary ring to it," Fitger said.

"Goddammit, Jay." He could almost hear her gritting her teeth. Just ahead of him, near a statue of Julius Agricola, Xanna had knelt to retie her shoe. She wore steel-toed boots that might have belonged to a construction foreman. All the accoutrements of ferocity, he thought. She had barely spoken to him for a week.

Janet was talking but the connection was bad, and Fitger was struggling to hold on to his phone and his audio guide and his umbrella. "You haven't formally accepted the job," he said, "so this entire discussion is premature."

Janet said it was *not* premature, it was called making plans and thinking one step ahead, and if he would stop for two seconds to—

The phone cut her off when he walked through a doorway and down a set of stone steps, where a placard informed him that Bath's hot springs were created "for the use of mortals" by Minerva, goddess of wisdom, law, medicine, commerce, weaving, and the arts. A sizable job description, he thought. He yawned.

His phone rang; it was Janet. Had Fitger hung up on her?

No; he was learning about the people of Aquae Sulis. Wasn't it time for Janet to be getting ready for work?

No, it was Sunday.

Well. So it was. He had lost track. He walked through the exhibits—here was a Gorgon's head, here a collection of Roman coins—while recalling that Sunday mornings, for Janet, typically involved either tennis or yoga, and sometimes both. Even on weekends, her habits were salubrious and as regular as a clock's. She woke at six-fifteen every morning, and the first thing she did after climbing out of bed was to reach for the ceiling, then touch her fingertips (and, on particularly auspicious mornings, the palms of her hands) to the floor. Fitger pictured the backs of her knees with their lovely architectural tendons, the purple vein in her left thigh like the letter Z. Her voice was cutting in and out; he missed every third word.

"You don't . . . him very much," she said. ". . . never say . . . friendly . . . or anything . . . about him."

He yawned again, feeling a touch of indigestion. He assumed she was talking about the dog and the extent to which Fitger praised or seemed to enjoy him. There was little to admire in Rogaine's fetid breath and fanged expression, or in the daily collection of his coils of shit, the dog standing by, impatient, while Fitger gathered the steaming burden; but human beings had their drawbacks, too. "I don't think he minds what I say about him. His grasp of English is tentative."

While following the students through another doorway, he missed Janet's response. Now they had reached the bath itself—a pool of gray-green water, curls of sulfurous steam rising up from its surface. His thoughts felt glutinous and slow, as if he were hauling them effortfully into his brain. "Can I make a suggestion?" he asked.

Janet said she would rather hit herself in the head with a tire iron than hear his suggestion.

"Excuse me. Sir? You're blocking the walkway."

Fitger turned and saw before him a Roman centurion wearing a metal breastplate and a bright red broom-like crest, like a brushy coxcomb, on his head. He had always found it difficult to respect an adult in a costume, but he stepped to the side.

155

"My suggestion," he told Janet, "is that Rogaine stay with me during the summers and during the academic breaks. The long weekends. We'll arrange for him to go back and forth."

On Janet's end of the line, he heard a door open; she was probably letting the dog out to do his morning business. "You know it's too far for us to drive him back and forth."

Fitger calculated the distance. It was a six- to seven-hour ride from Payne to Chicago, thirteen hours round trip. An image of their piebald mutt clutching a hobo's stick-and-handkerchief by the side of the highway floated into his mind. "Maybe he can take the train," he said, as a wave of fatigue washed through his limbs.

The centurion had made a lap around the pool and now pointed, with a sandaled foot, to the umbrella that had slid from Fitger's grasp. Its wrist strap had broken; Fitger collected the apparatus, and the centurion resumed his promenade. Janet was insisting that Fitger didn't love Rogaine for the dog's own sake; his motive was spite. Wasn't he trying to stake a claim only to punish her?

Fitger leaned against a pillar, resting his eyes. Rogaine was ill-tempered and only occasionally obedient, and he had an appetite for the heels of leather shoes. But the day before Fitger left for England, he was doing errands with the dog, who, sitting shotgun, had pressed the button on the armrest that rolled down his window so that he could bare his teeth at other drivers in their cars. He had growled with particular intensity at a professor of economics when they stopped at a light, with a discernment that Fitger found truly impressive. He hadn't shared that anecdote with Janet because she wouldn't approve.

His audio guide, hanging on a string around his neck, had somehow developed a mind of its own and was spouting information about previous sections of the museum, sharing, at increasing volume, its knowledge about John Wood the Elder and John Wood the Younger, architects, and father and son.

"Jay? Are you listening?" Janet asked.

The centurion was back. He reached for the audio guide and shut it off with a click. Fitger noted the size of the man's forearms, folded in front of his chest like two slabs of meat. Would Fitger mind stepping away from the Roman column, as it wasn't erected two thousand years ago so that he and his filthy raincoat could lean against it?

Stowing his phone away in a pocket, Fitger informed the centurion that his coat wasn't filthy. It was probably cleaner than the leather underpants that the centurion was presumably wearing.

Ha! Americans were such comedians, the centurion said. He reached for Fitger's arm in an effort to remove him from the Roman column, perhaps accidentally, in the process, squeezing Fitger's bandaged right hand. Fitger responded by—also perhaps accidentally—using his left hand to cuff the centurion's stubbled chin. An apology was tendered, but it did not suffice. A lanky young man dressed as a shepherd joined the centurion in escorting Fitger away from the baths and into a windowless office. There he waited incommunicado for nearly an hour, until a woman with a clipboard and a ladder down the leg of her stocking woke him with a tap on the back of his head and delivered a halting, monotonous lecture regarding modes of behavior that compromised the safety, enjoyment, or well-being of employees or visitors to the

Roman Baths. Would Mr. Fitsler agree not to visit the baths again during his time in England? Yes, he agreed. She asked him to sign his name and then let him go.

Out on the street, it was drizzling and nearly evening. The students were waiting for him on the other side of a small stone plaza, across from the pump room and the baths. The air felt wet and thick as he walked toward them, each breath he took as if sieved through a cloud. The undergrads were surprisingly quiet, perhaps anxious to hear about the jail cell in which he'd been imprisoned, and what penalties, if any, he'd had to pay. Obviously, some sort of explanation was in order, as it wasn't every day of the week that students saw their professor engage in a brawl with an historical figure.

He took a breath and tried to gather his thoughts. He began by confessing to the students that he had never liked England. He had agreed to serve as their chaperone only under duress. The trip was poorly planned from the start; furthermore, his own performance, as instructor, was clearly subpar. The students would have been better off, he said, with someone more energetic. Someone younger, someone who would have managed to keep track of eleven students, and who would not have started off the term by falling down a set of stairs or ended it with a wrestling match at the Roman Baths. He apologized for babbling. He had been given to understand that he was not a nurturing or well-socialized person. And it had been—he was sure the students would agree—a stressful three weeks. Each of them, he knew, had suffered their own individual struggles, and he regretted deeply the possibility that he had aggravated instead of assuaged them. He offered no excuses; he was a lonely, blundering man in the twilight years of an undistinguished career.

The students were silent. Had they never seen a grown man, a professor, unravel in front of them? Well, it was time they broadened their perspectives. Fitger apologized again for his rambling and his inattentiveness. He wasn't feeling well and he'd been distracted by a personal issue during their tour of the baths. The fact that the students had witnessed his altercation with a Roman centurion was—

"Mrs. Gray died," Lin said.

Fitger noticed for the first time that the audio guide still dangled from its string around his neck. "Mrs. Gray?"

"Her cat." Joe Ballo nodded toward to Felicity. "She got a call from her mom."

"Oh. Of course. Mrs. Gray." He found a handkerchief in his pocket; he was sweating; he wiped the damp from his neck. "I'm sorry to hear that." Though not personally acquainted with Mrs. Gray, Fitger understood that she had been well loved and that she had lived, in cat years, to a ripe old age. In a recent, widely shared video, he had seen her devour a generous portion of shredded cheese. "I'm very sorry." He looked at Felicity, who stood between Elwyn and Lin. He didn't realize at first that she was crying because she wasn't making any noise; there was no trembling of shoulders, no gasping breath. Moving closer, though, as the other students drew back in front of him, he saw the two tributaries of tears, twin silent rivers of grief traversing her face. She was clutching something in her hand: the feline raincoat, its price tags still attached and dangling down.

He took another step toward her, mindful as always of the protocol: there was no embracing of students, young female students in particular, but his arms seemed to have made a decision of their own as he approached, because he recognized that tolling bell of grief that rang in the chest. How to live with sadness and pain: here was a question that literature had treated for years and never satisfactorily answered. Felicity had loved Mrs. Gray; she had loved a twelve-pound nonverbal creature who shat in a plastic box full of gravel. Inexplicable, and yet Fitger understood it, the knowledge of it shivered through him, and when he put his arms around Felicity he felt her sadness travel like a balm through them both. He embraced her, his injured right hand gently clasping her shoulder while his left . . .

Something had happened to his left arm. Felicity was leaning against him (or perhaps he was leaning against her?), and the audio guide seemed to have tightened its hold around his neck, which made it difficult to breathe. The air had thickened, and the unsettledness in his stomach had turned into a pressure on his chest, his left arm becoming a causeway for bolts of lightning that caromed between shoulder and wrist.

"Professor Fitger?" someone asked. "Are you okay?"

He wasn't sure how to answer.

"Guys? I think something's wrong with him. Professor Fitger?"

I never said goodbye to Janet, Fitger thought. *I never ended our call.*

"Move back; give him room. Hey, Professor Fitger! Hey! Can you hear me?"

TEN

SONIA MORALES

FINAL ESSAY
WINTER BREAK—EXPERIENCE ENGLAND

Note to whoever is grading this:
I have completed my final assignment for this class as an inter-view like if someone was asking me about the time I was in England. Our professor told us we should strive for originality so I assume that's okay. Also we never did teacher evaluations in this class and I thought we were supposed to do them for every class. I would appreciate a chance to express my opinions.

An Interview with Sonia Morales

Hi, Sonia, tell us about your English experience.

Okay, well to be honest, my experience in England was a challenge. I had not been out of the US before except for a trip to Canada which is pretty much the same thing. My adviser in the Communications Department (I am a Communications major with a 3.4 GPA) said that part of getting an education is interacting with different cultures and that's why I came. But there were personal reasons that made this trip hard and also I don't like English food, especially the mashed-up peas in the dorm.

What did you see and do in England?

I saw Westminister Abbey and Big Ben and Parlament and a lot of other things in London that you usually only see on postcards. And we went to Oxford and Bath and to a lot of museums. We also did a lot of reading and had our grammar corrected. Personally, I do not think grammar should count so much in what is supposed to be a writing class.

Okay, Sonia, maybe try to get over yourself. ☺ Can you tell us what you will remember most and maybe focus on specific details, because that's what your professor was always telling you to do?

Haha, yeah. The part of the trip I will remember most is the Tower of London. I was never interested in history but being in the tower and hearing about the people who had their heads cut off (one of them got chased around the lawn by a guy with an axe) made it all come alive. Two of the prisoners were little boys, which is really sad. I forget their names, but one of them was scheduled to turn into a king, and they were both killed. Somebody found their bones a long time later, they were tossed altogether like old clothes in a dryer.

To be honest I am not a person who likes museums (I usually think they are boring) but this one didn't seem like it was trying to force me to learn anything, which I thought was good.

Can you give even more details, Sonia, and be even more specific than that.

Yes. For an example, our tour guide at the Tower of London was a man in a red suit called a Meat-Eater or a Warden, and he talked a lot about the ravens that are kind of like the royalty mascots. There are six ravens, with an extra bird in a cage in case one of them dies or flies away, and a legend about them says that if they ever disappear the tower will fall. I guess it is proving the point about specific details to say that a single raven can tell you more about history and superstition than a whole flock of robins can.

For other observations I would also describe the Traitor's Gate because being loyal or being a traitor is something I have thought a lot about during this trip. When you are going out with someone you have known since the seventh grade and he hooks up with a girl from your class and then expects that everything will be fine because he gave you a ring with a hair in its stone, that is something you think about a lot.

Most of the time I have been with Brent he has been a "good catch." (That is my mom's phrase. She has told me that if I break up with him someone else will snap him up and I will be left knitting a scarf in my dorm room alone.)

Maybe we should go back to the Tower of London, because you are supposed to be writing about a place that you visited.

I know but the assignment said we should relate the place to our own experience.

Okay I will mention the crown jewels, which are amazing all-and-all, but whatever you write about them has probably been said a hundred times.

The other part of the Tower that I will mention is the White Tower. This is where prisoners were kept (some of them had nice rooms but some slept in dungeons) and where a bunch of them were tortured. The Meateater Warden made a joke about instruments of torture having women's names. Like the Iron Maiden and the Scavenger's Daughter and the Duke of Exeter's Daughter, which either pulled people apart or twisted them into terrible positions, such as folded-in-half. Some people (Brent) laughed but I didn't think it was funny, that is when I got upset and walked away.

Can you explain why you were upset?

Yes. I got upset by looking at the torture tools because one of my favorite movies is *The Princess Bride* (to be honest I am kind of obsessed with it, Brent and I used to watch it in his basement), and there is a scene in the movie when the Wesley character is being electrified on a rack, and Inigo Montoya and the Giant hear him and recognize that he is not just screaming because of the torture but because of True Love.

And in the tower I was going to remind Brent of that part in the movie and our watching it with his little brother (who is really cute, he's only ten) but when he laughed about the torture tools I thought about his sleeping with the girl in our Chem 101 who had her leg cut off (because of her grades) and I thought forget it, True Love is bullshit, it is something you only see on the screen.

Is that when you started crying in front of those two old ladies from Australia?

Yeah, they were both really nice. I loved their accents. One

164

of them said she watched *The Princess Bride* with her grandson. She gave me a tissue and told me I should have worn a warmer coat (my warm one is ugly, green is not a good color for my complexion) and she said that a torture room was not the right place to think about love.

The other Australian lady got off track, talking about people being tortured today, even in the US. It seemed like she was saying I shouldn't be crying about me and Brent when the prisoners in the tower got twisted into shapes with metal bars or had their eyes scooped out with hot spoons but I couldn't help it. Plus, that was hundreds of years before I was born.

Your professor told you to expand your vocabulary and incorporate at least two new words into this essay. What are your words?

The first one (I found it in the online thesaurus) is dolorous which describes the way I felt during parts of this trip because of Brent. Dolorous means sorrowful, which is weird because I have an aunt named Dolores (she is my mom's older sister, they look just alike except my aunt dies her hair) and it never occurred to me until now that her name in Spanish means sadness or pain. My parents grew up speaking Spanish but they didn't teach it to us kids and believe me it can be embarrassing to have a name like Sonia Morales and not be able to say anything other than *Como Estas* and *Pendejo*.

The other word is coccyx, which is where tails would attach if humans walked on all fours.

Starting to bring this essay/interview to a conclusion, what advice do you have for other Payne students who might want to study with Experience: England?

I would tell them to come here on their own and not with a boyfriend or (worse) a possible future ex-boyfriend.

I would also tell them to find out if the actual class they signed up for is going to happen or if there would be a change at the last minute, like a different professor filling in and assigning much more work than the students thought they should have. I am not being critical, I am just saying that when a student is paying more than eight hundred dollars for a trip (I got a part scholarship, most people paid more) it should be the trip that was advertised. But that is just my own view.

You are certainly entitled to it. Here is our last question, Sonia, because I think you have described your time in England really well. Let's say ten years from now when maybe you have a house and a job and two kids, what would you say is the main thing you learned from this trip?

That is a good question, and I definitely like thinking about that kind of thing, I mean about the Sonia who I am right now and the Sonia I was ten years ago and the Sonia I will be in the future. I like to think about all those different Sonias together. Like if someone blew a whistle and a hundred or a thousand Sonia Moraleses stopped what they were doing and looked up from the piece of life they were living in and waved at each other—the Sonia in the high chair and the Sonia at her first Communion and the Sonia at the beach with Brent when she was wearing that bathing suit with the yellow ruffle, and the Sonia at her wedding and the old lady Sonia in the nursing home. They would all hear the whistle and it would be like a time-out in a football game, with all the different Sonias stopping what they were doing to look up and recognize each other. And each of them would be able to tell the other Sonias what they knew.

Maybe that is a weird idea but for some reason it makes me feel better. And right now while I am writing this paper I am thinking about all the other Sonias cheering me on, and most of them, especially the older ones, are saying *Fuck Brent Schraft* because you can find another boyfriend, or if you don't want to find one and you feel like knitting in your dorm room by yourself that is your choice and not your mother's, she will just have to deal.

Thanks very much for your time, Sonia!

Thanks. I have never written an essay like this before and I thought it was fun.

"*Fun.* Well, to each her own, I suppose. Jay? Are you with me? I can't tell if you're listening."

Fitger opened his eyes. He'd been struggling to emerge from multiple layers of sleep, a sort of underworld of dreams; he wondered if the vision of Janet Matthias, a stack of paper in her lap in the corner of his hospital room, would wink out like a dying star and disappear.

His chest hurt, and so did his head. The sheet and blanket that covered him felt as if they'd been weighted with stones.

"Since late last night," Janet said. "That's when I landed in London. And, yes, you're still in Bath." Fitger had an oxygen mask on his face and didn't remember asking her a question, but she was answering as if he had.

"We've already been over this a few times, but we might as well do it again." She set the stack of paper aside and picked up a Styrofoam cup of coffee. "You had a heart attack. And you seem to have a mild concussion—you hit your head. They're planning to let you out of here tomorrow, but you aren't supposed to fly for four or five days."

On the other side of a hanging curtain, Fitger heard someone moan.

"That's your roommate, Mrs. Antony," Janet said. "She has two parakeets and plays canasta. Anyway, the plan at this point is that once you're discharged, we'll go back to London. I booked two hotel rooms near Paddington, and they weren't cheap. I changed your plane ticket, too—you'll have some explaining to do about the budget when you get home."

Fitger pulled off his oxygen mask. "But how . . . you weren't . . ." He felt moony, his mind freckled with fog.

"You want to know who told me what happened? Lin Snow," Janet said. "She was an intern in my office last summer. She texted me to report that her professor was lying in the street and she and the other students were watching him die." Janet stood, looking down at him where he lay on his back, and sipped her coffee. "I gather most of them knew, presumably because you told them—for reasons I don't want to think about right now—that we were once married."

Fitger murmured an ambiguous dissent. Had he talked to the students about Janet? And where were they now?

Gone back to Payne, Janet said. She looked at her watch. She had traveled to the airport with them at six in the morning; they would be getting back to campus in a couple of hours.

Fitger managed to locate and press the button that raised the head of his bed. The move caused a pounding in his temples. But why hadn't the Experience: Abroad office—

"Because that office consists of three employees," Janet said, "one of whom had already been dispatched to a different crisis, one of whom was prohibitively pregnant, and one—in an international studies program—who lacked a valid passport. So, in the absence of other immediate possibilities, I volunteered."

Fitger blinked. He was struggling to keep up with the conversation and to accommodate the idea that his ex-wife, who hated England and felt a similar antipathy for the person to whom she had once been married, had flown to the U.K., tended to his (presumably shell-shocked) undergrads, and taken the train from London to sit beside him in a hospital room in Bath. "I hope you didn't have to pay for your flight."

"Of course not." Janet played doubles tennis with some of the senior staff in Accounting, who had handled the paperwork for her trip. These same accountants were the ones who required that Fitger submit forms in triplicate when requesting reimbursement for a bottle of water or a pencil or pen.

He listened to Janet explain that she'd packed up his things in Barking and had most of them sent to the hotel near Paddington Station. The Trout had helped; he needed the room because another group would soon be moving into the dorm. Janet zipped up her coat. She had brought Fitger an overnight bag. It was in the closet. She didn't want him traveling back to London in his lovely blue gown.

When he didn't answer, she picked up his oxygen mask and pressed it—a bit firmly, he thought—over his mouth and his nose. "That's a nice-looking bruise." She touched his brow.

He ran his fingers over the tender spot near his left temple. "I don't remember hitting my head," he said, his voice muffled because of the mask. "Did I fall?"

"Onto a curbstone," Janet said. "Though it seems the heart attack came first." She finished her coffee and set her cup down. She had been awake for twenty-two hours, she said, and she needed to eat and sleep and go for a walk. "Should I leave these here?" she asked.

"What are they?" Fitger shaded his eyes; the overhead light was too bright.

"Your students' essays. Never mind; you'd probably lose them. I'll be back tomorrow."

After she left, he dozed and woke and dozed again, still occasionally wondering if he had imagined his ex-wife's visit. But here was evidence: the paper coffee cup on the table beside him with a trace of lipstick—Deep Sienna, the shade she had worn for years—on the rim.

JOSEPH N. BALLO

PROFESSOR FITGER'S CLASS: FINAL PAPER

Of all the things we have seen during our time in England the one I have decided to write about is the Churchill War Rooms. I had heard of the War Rooms probably in school in a history class but had forgot about them before we came here. I have always been interested in the history of World War Two because I come from a military family my great grandfather wounded in Operation Torch my grandfather serving two tours in Vietnam. When I was younger I had hoped to enroll in ROTC.

In this essay we are supposed to write about something we have seen or experienced in England and at the same time tell what we were thinking while we had that experience. I am not sure how to do both of those things at one time so I will handle them by dividing my page in half the top half or section being dedicated to what I saw in the War Rooms and the bottom to what I was thinking while we were there.

One of the things I was thinking about in the Churchill War Rooms is my family's relationship to war. My great grandfather as I said fought in combat in World War Two I don't remember him well when he died I was four. I am not sure of the year he enlisted but he was wounded in the 168th Infantry and came home blind in one eye in 1943. Wearing a patch on that eye he teased me saying he was a pirate which is the main thing I remember about him. He was my grandfather on my mother's side.

Something about the war rooms I overlooked, I did not realize until we went down the stairs that this museum is not a good idea for a person who has a problem with enclosed spaces. The ceilings are low and the hallways are narrow, the entire museum is one hundred feet below street level under the ground. I blame myself, there is no one else that could be blamed. I should have known ahead of time that this was a bunker.

We went down the steps and into the first room. I was starting to get that closed-in feeling because there were no windows it is a hard-to-breath feeling you feel in your chest.

I did not always have a problem with small spaces it is something that happened to me like a trauma when I was fourteen. Before that time I was not afraid of much. When I went to juvenile detention I had to talk to a counselor once a month he knew I was claustrophobic, he said the small underground place we are all afraid of is the grave because even if we don't know we are thinking about it it is a subconscious fear. But I am not afraid of graves there is no use being afraid of what will happen to one-and-all the grave is the place we will eventually lie. I have visited my family's graves when I was young not only my grandmother's in Sturgis near the Black Hills but those of other relatives too. My mother is buried in Wisconsin near where we lived but I have not visited that place for almost four years.

I wanted to turn around and go back out the entrance but we had to keep moving because of another group had come into the museum just behind. There were documents to read on the walls and recordings to listen to from the time of the war. I wanted to read them, I had been looking forward to the museum but I could feel the blood running in then out of my face and my heart beating hard I needed to know where the exit was.

The trauma that happened to me is something that I have been told will always be with me it is like a chapter in a book you can't take it out but other chapters will be written later so it will take up less room. It is a dark chapter, it occurred when I was fourteen actually it was a week after the day I turned fourteen I remember it well. My mother died the year before (it was cancer of the lungs, she smoked) and my father never being married to her and not around I was moved to the home of my aunt and uncle and cousin, my cousin Roddy being four years younger than me at that time he just turned ten. They lived in South Dakota in the house that belonged to my grandfather at one time, this was my mother's father who fought in Vietnam. When he came back after two years service he bought a house with a fallout shelter in the side yard. My mother said he was damaged because of the war. The shelter was big enough for three or maybe four people with a bunkbed and shelves for canned food. It was musty but cool. My aunt and uncle didn't use it they considered it like extra storage but my cousin Roddy an only child (both of us were) used to sometimes play together down there.

I did not want to panic or push but the not-breathing feeling was getting stronger and I saw darkness like a tunnel beginning to close at the edge of my eyes. It was a feeling of shame at the same time because my grandfather and great-grandfather both fought overseas a point of pride in the family I come from but I was afraid of a museum about the war.

Roddy and I were down in the shelter we were hanging out, he had some of my uncle's cigarettes. I told him not to be stupid, if he was going to smoke down here they will smell the smoke on your clothes. My mother had died of cancer as I said. I grabbed the matches my cousin wanted them back. He said he was tired of me bossing him around. I liked Roddy but he had a temper I think it was hard on him that I had moved in with his family he was used to being a kid on his own. He had a gun in the shelter from his dad's truck it was not a twelve gauge like we were used to it was a handgun and he was pissed about the matches trying to show that I wasn't in charge, he waved it around. I have known about guns my whole life, my mother went with a man for a while he knew about guns. I went to grab this gun from my cousin. There is a piece of time after that that I can't recall all I remember is the two of us wrestling. Then Roddy was lying on the floor with a ring of blood around his mouth, he was calling to me. I saw the stairs to the shelter but Roddy was in front of them his mouth with the ring of blood calling my name. I must have climbed out but I

I knew I was in trouble I was thinking I might pass out my heart beating fast when Xanna one of the other students in our group took hold of my arm. She said to keep breathing and she would walk with me and if I needed to shut my eyes that was okay because she would tell me what was in front of us and what she saw. She talked softly holding onto my arm and said Churchill and the people in World War Two worked and stayed down here but we are just visiting, you can keep your eyes closed she said, here is the room where Churchill talked to Roosevelt, there are the clunky old fashion phones, here is the war room with the clock stopped on the wall, now I am looking at the kitchen where someone cooked for them and made all their meals. She described the things that were in front of us as if I could see them it was a kindness I will hope sometime to repay.

---

don't remember that part, I was told later that I climbed the stairs with the gun in my hand. I never saw my cousin again. At first the doctors said he might live but they were wrong. I had a law-yer appointed by the court and spent eighteen months in juvenile detention it was manslaughter, the worst year and a half I have lived so far. My aunt and uncle could not keep me with them after that which is understandable there is no blame on my part and that is when I went to foster care. It was an accident my uncle said, but Roddy was a younger boy and I was his older cousin, he was just ten. It was hard for my aunt in particular to be anywhere near me she had trouble even seeing my face. In the past few years I have seen them only two times.

With Xanna leading me and talking I was not exactly calm but I did feel better the claustrophobia not as oppressive, her voice was a string I was following to get through the museum.

I left the Churchill museum following Xanna we stood together out on the street where it was good to feel the light of day. I caught my breath. I told her some things about myself, about the difficulties I had experienced we all have our share. She talked about some of her troubles too I won't name them here but she has had her own challenges. I thanked her for helping me through the museum.

I have been told that over time I will make new memories so the memory of the underground shelter will fade. But in my experience a bad memory is always there, it is like a basement in your house, even if you don't open the door or walk down those steps it is always there.

Professor Fitger I apologize for the underside of my essay taking up more room than I intended and I know this is shorter than you said it should be. I hope you are okay and you get this essay. Also I know you told me to use more commas in my writing and I am trying to fit them in but I am still, unsure, about where they should go.

"Joseph N. Ballo," Janet said. She was back, as promised, seated in the corner of Fitger's hospital room. "The poor thing. It doesn't seem that his professor was of much use to him in the museum."

"His professor was probably busy with some other catastrophe," Fitger said. He felt a bit more alert, but the bruise on his temple was the size and color of a plum and the walls of his room, when he sat up, had a tendency to swerve as if he'd boarded a ship. He found it impossible to read. He told Janet that he worried that his brain had been damaged: he remembered nothing about the ambulance ride or his arrival at the hospital, and even the hour or two prior to his heart attack was hazy and muddled. Of his time in the Roman Baths he recalled only snapshots out of sequence: a woman with a ladder in her stocking, a husky, costumed fool near a body of water, and a display case full of ancient coins.

"That's the concussion," Janet told him. "Headache, fatigue, blurred vision." She pointed out that he might have expired on the sidewalk or under the surgeon's blood-spattered gloves, but here he was, tucked comfortably into clean sheets. He had given up the oxygen mask and managed a bowl of tepid oatmeal. So: Progress. Step-by-step. All would eventually, she supposed, be well.

Would it, though? Fitger covered one eye with the palm of his hand and then the other. What if the dizziness didn't recede? Already his heart had revealed itself to be temperamental, and there were gaps in his memory like the holes in Swiss cheese. What if he had lost the ability to think coherently? What if he had—

Janet interrupted to point out that he hadn't lost the ability to be a pain in the ass. And as for his memory, if he wanted to know what had happened when he hit his head, someone named Wyatt Franklin could tell him. She opened the folder in her lap and skimmed through it. "Here it is: 'A Moment I Will Remember from Our Experience: England Class.'" She turned the pages of the essay. "Let's see. You're looking peaked so I'll skip the introduction, which is his long-winded way of saying he hopes you're still alive. Okay, page three: 'Our professor was sweating. He wiped the sweat but it kept coming. It was pouring off him like a waterfall on a hillside of flesh.' This student is fond of metaphor. He goes on to say that your knees 'bent in half like a horse when it tries to sit down.' Very visual. And, here's my favorite part: the sound when your head hit the curb was that of 'another rock hitting a rock.'"

"Okay, ouch," Fitger said.

"Apparently your skull actually bounced," Janet told him.

They heard a knock at the door. Dr. Ravanni, a petite young woman Fitger might have mistaken for one of his students, introduced herself, plugged a stethoscope into her ears, raised Fitger's bed to a sitting position, and swiftly untied the strings at the back of his gown.

Propped upright, he felt dizzy again, and utterly naked, as he hadn't since changing into a bathing suit for swimming class when he was thirteen.

"Any discomfort? Pain or pressure?" the doctor asked.

"What?" The doorway in front of him swayed back and forth and, looking down, he was distracted by the sight of the hair on his chest, which was thick and nearly white, his sagging nipples protruding through the fur like an orangutan's.

"He isn't known for stoicism when it comes to anything medical," Janet said, "so you would definitely hear from him if he was in pain."

The doctor smiled.

"My heart stopped beating," Fitger said, closing one eye to keep the vertigo at bay. The word "pressure" had revived in him the sensation of lying on his back on the cold damp stone, a clamor of voices overhead.

"No, that would be cardiac arrest. Not heart attack." The doctor's stethoscope made its way through the lawn on his chest. Cardiac arrest, she explained, meant the sudden cessation of heart function, as well as breathing and circulation; what had happened to him was a clot.

Fine. He stood corrected. Still, his heart, which had been thumping away behind the louvered doors of his ribs for decades, had tossed a flag into the air and issued a warning; the next time it might decide to end the game.

He asked about dizziness and was told that it would resolve over time. Then he listened to a description of the incision in his groin that had served as an entry for two coronary stents that were keeping his clogged arteries open. Thus far Mr. Fitger (the doctor turned toward Janet) was reacting well. She asked about family history of cardiac problems or respiratory distress.

"Not that we know of," Janet said, because Fitger had been slow to respond. Still parsing the heart attack vs. cardiac arrest distinction, he was simultaneously trying to remember the name of the third sister of Fate, the one with the scissors. Did it start with an *A*? Was it an indication of brain damage if he couldn't remember?

The doctor examined the bruise on his head, then pulled up his gown and retied its strings.

"Atropos!" Fitger said.

The doctor nodded and turned toward Janet again. Confusion and fatigue, she said, were common after heart attack, as well as concussion. Rest was important. She would send Fitger home with some reading material, and he should check with his primary physician in the U.S. about return to exercise and to work. The hospital would keep him for observation, just to be safe, for one more day.

Janet thanked her, and Dr. Ravanni tucked her stethoscope into her pocket. She shook Janet's hand. Sexual intercourse following a heart attack, she said, could typically be resumed in three to four weeks.

"I'll be sure to warn the women he comes in contact with," Janet said.

The doctor apologized; she had thought they were married.

"Unhappily divorced," Fitger said.

"After having been unhappily married," Janet added, "for eleven years."

Dr. Ravanni left them and moved on to Mrs. Antony behind the curtain; they heard her ask about the patient's bowels.

"That must be my cue," Janet said. "I'll come back tomorrow to pick you up. Let me know what time I should order a cab."

"Wait," Fitger said. He didn't want her to go. "We were talking about your job offer," he said. "At the Roman Baths. And talking about Rogaine. We got disconnected."

"Right. But we're not going into that while you're still in the hospital." Janet looked at her watch. She'd scheduled a tour of the Jane Austen Centre that began in an hour.

"You said you were going to meet with a realtor," Fitger said. He pointed out that Rogaine was used to doing his business out in the yard. But a yard in Chicago would be expensive. Did her realtor think that—

"I canceled the meeting with the realtor so I could fly to London," Janet said.

"Oh. Right." Fitger tugged at a snag in his cotton gown. "So you'll reschedule for when you get back. But before you do, we should talk about the—"

Janet stood up. "We're not doing this now, Jay. We're not going to discuss Chicago or the fate of the dog."

Gingerly, he nodded, conscious of the bump on his head. "Did you have to leave him at the canine spa?"

The last time they had both been out of town and had no other options, they'd booked Rogaine into a "pet wellness resort" which offered therapeutic massage and had two swimming pools, but the dog had let them feel his displeasure for the perceived abandonment, behaving in a theatrical manner when they brought him home.

"The spa was booked," Janet said. "So I left him with Fran. She's planning to bring him to your office this week while she works. I told her you'd reimburse her for any damage to the furniture or to personnel."

"He's usually selective about the people he bites. And he's not as young and spry as he was." Fitger watched Janet gather her things. "You didn't finish reading the essay," he said. "You stopped in the middle and left me in suspense. On tenterhooks. I'm too dizzy to read it myself."

She paused in the doorway. "You're really going to milk this thing, aren't you?"

He was ready to remind her of all the times he'd read to her while she lay in the tub—but, no need: she sat down and crossed her legs and reopened the folder. "I think we left off with profuse sweating," she said. "Does that ring a bell?"

It did. He remembered: the air had been cold when he was finally released from the Roman Baths, but his face and his body had been clammy with sweat.

Our professor was on the sidewalk and people on the street were walking around like nothing happened. I knelt down next to him and touched his face and said I think you are having a heart attack, have you had one before?

"Strange." Fitger lowered the head of his bed and closed his eyes. "I don't remember that at all."

I said my name and I told him he was doing okay because it is important to keep the person calm. We called 911—the number is different in England, it is 999—and I went through his pockets because he might have had nitroglycerin. I found his wallet and his phone and a travel-size bottle of aspirin. I chewed up one of the pills and smeared the chewed up bits in his mouth. Joe Ballo helped me prop the professor up, the best thing is having knees bent and something propping up the head and shoulders. The professor's eyes were still open, maybe he was wondering why his student was feeding him something he had just taken out of his mouth. I kept talking, I knew he had hit his head hard on the way down and I thought maybe I will be the last thing in his life he will see.

"It's very dramatic," Janet said. "Are you still awake?"

Fitger gave her a soporific thumbs-up.

I wasn't sure the ambulance was near but I told him it was. I told him he was going to be fine. When the medics showed up everything happened really fast, they asked his name and loaded him onto the stretcher. He wasn't talking anymore. They told us the name of the hospital and turned on the siren and drove away.

"If you're going to snore," Janet said, "I'll skip to the end. It's eleven pages."

"I wasn't snoring," Fitger said.

"Okay, let's see, page ten. They took the bus back to London and went to a pub."

. . . which is something we didn't usually all do together, to go to the Swans, but nobody wanted to be by themselves. Lin was still texting with someone from Payne—

"That must have been you," Fitger said.

—and Joe Ballo was checking with the hospital but they didn't have news. We ordered a pitcher and food and we talked. There are things we learned about each other that night at the Swans that we wouldn't have found out anywhere else.

Xanna was next to me eating olives speared in a row on a plastic sword. She said, You knew what to do. How did you know about the aspirin?

I told her that I am a Wilderness First Responder (I am certified). But also it was a coincidence about the aspirin because that morning maybe ten hours earlier our professor opened that bottle and gave an aspirin to me. Sonia was listening, she said it was amazing the way things lined up sometimes it must have been Fate and our professor was lucky. She looked at me and said, Just think if you had gone to the Caribbean instead.

We went back to the dorm really late and I was tired but couldn't sleep. So I got out of bed to write this essay, and it is strange to say that while I was writing it I felt better than I have in a while. Because it is true that I knew how to help, and I will always remember our professor looking at me with his half open eyes when I fed him the aspirin. I think he remembered that I am a Certified First Responder. And I might not have saved a life, but I tried.

ELEVEN

During their three days in London, while waiting for his brain to allow him to fly, Fitger didn't see much of Janet. She claimed she was touring the city or working. Besides, she said, he was clearly teetering at the edge of complete exhaustion: he had slept on the train from Bath, then sacked out on a couch in the lobby of their hotel while Janet checked them into their rooms. So she left him alone during the day; but every evening she stopped by to see how he felt: How was the heart, and how was the head?

The heart appeared to be beating, he said, but the dizziness—an occasional spinning sensation—persisted. He could barely walk across the black-and-white-striped carpet in his room (an oddly vertiginous choice in hotel decor, in his opinion) without needing to reach for the back of a chair or the wall. Did she think his dizziness could be chalked up, in part, to shock, his mind and body reacting to the near-death experience?

Janet accused him of exaggeration. He was less dizzy now than he was in the hospital; he should stop looking at the striped carpet. "And no one said you were near death," she said, while plucking the grapes from his fruit salad. She had discovered the remains of his room-service meal. "Plenty of people have heart attacks. They aren't . . . exceptional."

Fitger, looking rumpled, was seated in bed amid a tangle of sheets. "You should probably look up the word 'exceptional,'" he said. "I wouldn't use it in reference to warts or swimmer's ear, but a heart attack—"

Janet interrupted to remind him that he hadn't suffered a cardiac arrest; he'd had a *clot*. "And why aren't you eating your fruit salad?"

"Because I don't like fruit salad. I never have. But no matter what I order, they keep sending it up with the rest of my food in those little cups." He watched her finish the fruit, her long fingers like tongs. "Can we talk about our plans for the dog now?" he asked.

She went into the bathroom to wash her hands. "No. We aren't going to do that yet."

"Why not?"

"Because," Janet said. "You're a person with a weak heart and a damaged brain, and you're supposed to be avoiding stress." She came out of the bathroom holding a sample-size bottle of shampoo. "You aren't using this?" She unscrewed the lid and sniffed the contents.

"I changed my mind about being brain-damaged," Fitger said. "And you were just lecturing me about heart attacks being trivial. I don't want to argue. I just want to be sure that we both—"

"We always argue, Jay. We can't help it. Ninety percent of the things we disagree about turn into a brawl. And if you antagonize me now, I'll go back to my room and leave you and your invalid body to fly home by yourself." She screwed the lid back onto the shampoo and dropped it into her purse. The folder of student essays was on the nightstand next to the bed. "Were you able to read them?" She pointed.

"No." He touched the lump on his head. "I get through a line or a paragraph, and then the words unfasten themselves from the page."

She perched on the edge of the bed and opened the folder. "This one's short and easy to read." She held it up. "It says, 'I don't need the credits. Thanks for a great class.' Succinct."

"That must be D.B." Fitger watched her fingers scrabble through the collection of pages. "Did you actually see him at the airport? Dark glasses? He might have been holding a boarding pass to Nairobi."

Janet didn't remember. She held up another final assignment. "Lin Snow. I'm not sure I would call hers an essay. It's more of a—"

"Diatribe?" Fitger asked.

"No, a petition. She wants the Experience: Abroad office to change everyone's grades in your class to pass/fail." She switched on the lamp and he noted the glow of light on her skin.

I am in the process of collecting signatures from the other ten enrolled students and will send them with another copy of this letter when we get back to Payne. When your instructor collapses on the street, his head hitting the pavement right in front of you, the usual A-to-F system shouldn't apply. Also the Experience Abroad office should be sued (I am applying to law school next year and can look into this) for not answering their *emergency phone.*

"It's a reasonable argument," Janet said.

Anything other than an A or a "Pass" would be unethical. And personally I can't afford to get a mediocre grade during my junior year. Ms. Matthias in the law school will vouch for me—

"True," Janet said.

—and has already promised to write one of my law school recommendations. If I need more than three letters for my application I will ask Professor Fitger to write one. If he gets out of the hospital, he will be one of my back-up plans.

"How very flattering." Fitger watched as she turned the page.

Your office is lucky that one of our classmates (who I always thought was kind of a fuck-up) knew CPR.

"Another good point. I would sign her petition," Janet said. "She goes on, in the next paragraph, to lodge a complaint about your obsession with the difference between 'lie' and 'lay.' Also the fact that you wouldn't let her use the word 'real.'"

"No. The prohibited word," Fitger said, "*one* of the prohibited words, was 'really.' Also 'important' and 'importantly,' both of which are insidious."

"Insidious." Janet straightened the bedspread. "It'll be interesting to see your teaching evaluations. 'My professor censored my speech. But I learned a lot when he nearly dropped dead at the Roman Baths.'"

Fitger turned toward her and caught a glimpse of himself in the mirror over the dresser: he looked like a hermit who had recently staggered out of a cave. "What if they didn't learn anything?" he asked. "Maybe I'm getting too old to teach. Do you think I'm too old?"

"You were always too old." Janet paged through the essays. "For as long as I've known you, you've been whining about the passage of time."

She knew him so well, Fitger thought. He reminded her that reading was a significant part of his job. If he couldn't read and comment on his students' work, they might as well ship him off to the Payne retirement home, populated by ancient emeriti faculty who could be found parked in their wheelchairs like a row of toadstools at the back of any lecture hall.

"Look; I like this one." Janet held up another essay. "And maybe it won't make you dizzy because there are very few words on each page." She showed him a postcard taped to a sheet of paper. *"The Cholmondeley Ladies,"* she said. She turned the page.

"The authors—two of them—are Andromeda and Cassiopeia. They apparently spent a lot of time at the Tate, thinking about twinness. Listen: 'We are thoroughly monozygotic, but with different birthdays, having entered the world on either side of midnight on June 3 and 4.' They can certainly draw. Did they do all their assignments together?"

Fitger studied the portrait while explaining to Janet that the Wagner-Halls had steadfastly ignored the prohibition, clearly stated in his syllabus, against collaborative work.

"Good for them—rules are meant to be broken," Janet said. "They go on to discuss the concept of the 'female gaze' as it relates to being an identical twin. 'The doubleness draws the eye but it's also a cloak. Being one half a two-of-a-kind can be a kind of disguise.' It's clever. And they're clearly talented." She showed him the next illustration.

Fitger covered one eye and considered it. "On a pass/fail basis, I can give that a pass," he said, "on condition that I never have to evaluate student artwork again."

"Funny you should say that," Janet said. "Because apparently they've written to Vivi Wayetu in Art and asked her to advise a semester-long Cholmondeley project. A hybrid, with image and text. They want to study female twinness. And Vivi's agreed. She's also approved the idea of Professor Fitger as co-adviser, because of the inclusion of text." On Janet's face, he saw the barest hint of a smile. He understood that his love for her would never be extinguished; for the rest of his life, it would have to be painfully survived.

"It wasn't spite, you know," he said. "You asked me if I wanted to keep the dog to punish you."

She looked away from him and put the essay back in its folder, and he admired the way that her clavicles protruded at the base of her neck. "It wasn't spite," he said again, and as he spoke, a few of the clouds in his memory cleared, and he remembered Felicity weeping, feline raincoat in hand, at the Roman Baths.

"It's getting late." Janet stood.

He watched her walk across the room. They hadn't spent time together like this for years. "If my vision doesn't improve, I could take a medical leave," he said.

Janet reminded him that the doctor said it would improve.

"But if it didn't, and I took a leave," he said, "I could rent an apartment in Chicago."

She had her hand on the doorknob. "You're joking."

Well, no, he wasn't joking. It would be a lot for her, he said, caring for the dog by herself. She would be busy with her new job; and she had to admit that she could get prickly when overwhelmed. What did she think? He could find something cheap and short-term, a couple of basement-level rooms, and she could leave the dog with him when she was at work.

"Jay. I don't want you following me to Chicago."

"I don't think 'following' is the right word," he said. "I'm trying to help. Isn't it possible that—"

"No." Janet turned toward him. "This is why I don't want to talk to you! I don't want to talk about the dog or about Chicago. I don't want to talk. At all. Because you are impossible. You are completely . . ." She clutched at her head. He heard her breathing, ragged, stertorous exhalations through her nose.

"Janet?" he asked. She was murmuring to herself, some sort of incantation or secular prayer. "I just—"

She held her hand up to stop him. Then, slowly, she bent down between the bed and the dresser and knelt on the rug. He watched while she opened the door of the mini-fridge.

"I'm going to have a drink," she said. "Do you want one? They have gin or vodka."

Of course he wanted one. Was he supposed to be drinking? He didn't remember being cautioned against it. Perhaps he *had* been cautioned against it, and that was her point. As for gin or vodka, he told her to choose.

She twisted the tops off two small bottles and, still kneeling, poured their drinks into two plastic cups. Fitger understood that it was best if he didn't speak, so they drank in silence for a few minutes, after which Janet said she intended to mentally erase his earlier, unfortunate remarks—they no longer existed—and she asked if he needed time to pack. Their flight was the next day at noon, which meant she would advocate for arrival at the airport at dawn.

Fitger assured her that he would be ready. It was startling, he thought, that in little more than twenty-four hours he would be back in his old life at Payne. Janet would be busy when they returned. She would have to pack up her house and rent it out, and by early spring when the Payne campus was especially bleak, snow thawing in ragged heaps on the quad, he would walk down one of the icy sidewalks in the direction of her office at the law school and suffer a pang of realization: she would be gone, and the last tie between them would have come undone. He would have to take up a hobby; perhaps he would learn to play mah jong.

Out in the hall, a woman was calling for someone named Zeke to hold the elevator. "I said, *Hold it for me!*" she screamed.

"You know, I haven't disliked England this time the way I

did when we came here together," Janet said, sitting back on her heels.

Fitger suggested that she might have enjoyed her visit, back then, if he'd checked into a hospital with a heart attack as soon as they arrived.

"I suppose that's possible." Janet shrugged.

"Zeke! You didn't *hold it*!" The woman in the hall was howling.

"It's been nice, having you read to me," Fitger said. "Speaking as a visually impaired person, I've been enjoying the sound of your voice. You have a good reading voice. Not too high or too low. It's very smooth."

Janet looked at her watch. "I could read you one more," she said, perhaps reluctantly, while gesturing toward the folder of essays. "I have some phone calls to make, but I can spare you an hour. Unless you're too tired?"

No. He wasn't tired. But about those phone calls: Would she be talking to people about the job in Chicago? Or to her realtor?

Janet pretended not to hear him. "This one is called 'In Westmonster Abbey.' A note at the top informs us that it's 'an essay in fiction form.'"

"Elwyn Yang," Fitger said. He patted the bed beside him, and Janet got up off the floor, brushed some dust from her knees, and sat.

When the ancient graves in the stone floor broke open, releasing their centuries-old dead, most of the American students who were visiting London from Payne University were in a little known cloister and didn't hear anything. Unbeknownst to them, they were the last visitors that day to Westminster (also known as Westmonster) Abbey, and the people in charge of the famous English church (which goes back to William the Conquerer 1,000 years ago) had forgotten that the unsuspecting foreign visitors were there. The old creepy old cathedral, which was ordered to be built in the Romanesque style by Edward the Confessor in 1065, was locked with the Americans inside.

"He's done his research," Janet said.

A legend about the gigantic eerie historic building said that at the stroke of 3:45 pm on certain Wednesdays, the famous dead kings and queens and other corpses would wake in their moldering graves and in the old blood-curdling style of earlier eras would hunt for revenge. You couldn't learn about it on a tourist website but it was well known. The sound of crackling graves and rolling stones from some of the 3,300 interments in the Abbey could not be denied. Panic went through the students like shit through a drain.

Fitger sipped at his drink. "Vivid."

The only student who stayed calm was Elwyn. He had seen every horror movie made in the past ten years and did all the reading for the class (on time). Some of the others didn't trust him, Elwyn was not exactly popular, he had a skin condition which was not his fault and was definitely not contagious but it kept him on the fringes of things anyway.

Janet briefly looked up. "I am *so* glad I'm not twenty years old."

By now the dead and desiccated bodies were coming up from their graves. Some of the corpses included royalty from the Henry VII Lady Chapel which was dedicated in 1503 and is known for its amazing fan-vaulted ceiling. Some of the people buried there are Elizabeth I and Mary Queen of Scots who was Catholic and whose head was cut off by her cousin; it took several blows with an axe.

Elwyn waited until he saw a person who had been dead for a very long time (he could tell because of her advanced putrefaction) who was by herself and he flagged her down. It turned out she was Aphra Behn who was a woman writer who he actually had to learn about during the previous semester at Payne. He told her he had read her in a class in the United States. She said she hadn't heard of the US because she was born in 1640 and died in 1689. They talked for a while. Elwyn told her about the American revolution and about his coming to study in England. When the small talk ran out Aphra pushed her eyeball back in its socket and suggested that Elwyn move out of the way and let her devour a few of his friends, because she knew they were hiding behind the big tomb.

Elwyn explained that the other students were not necessarily his friends, in fact most of them didn't want to hang out with him.

Really, what about that girl with the cat who you went to Kensington Gardens with? Aphra asked.

That was Felicity. Actually, her cat just died, Elwyn said.

Aphra who had once worked as a spy in the Netherlands and maybe even also South America said she was sorry about the cat.

"Aphra Behn was a spy in the Netherlands?" Janet asked.
"Not my area." Fitger shrugged.

They heard someone screaming behind the coronation chair, which was made of oak in 1308.

Aphra and Elwyn talked about the way that people can be rude and cliquish. Elwyn told her that in high school kids called him gator because of his skin. He showed her the rash on his arm.

Aphra pointed to the rotting strips of flesh like beef jerky hanging from her elbow. At least you don't have this problem, she said. She and Elwyn shared a laugh.

Janet's phone buzzed. She scowled at the screen.
"Do you need to get that?" Fitger asked.
"No. Later." She shut the phone off.

It turned out Aphra wasn't happy about the place she was buried. She was a writer and a pretty famous one (Elwyn had read about her in British Lit I) but instead of being buried with the big-name writers in Poet's Corner she had been rotting away in the east cloister under a plain black stone. It pissed her off. With the hunting and killing still going on around them she explained to Elwyn that Geoffrey Chaucer and Edmund Spenser and Samuel Johnson and other writers all got to be buried in Poet's Corner, the famous writers who were men hogging all the good spots. Even Thomas Hardy who wrote a book that totally sucked (Jude the Obscure) got to be there, but his heart was removed.

Elwyn was about to make a suggestion but just then another dead woman stumbled toward them with a human femur in her fist like a sword. The new dead woman turned out to be a friend of Aphra's whose name was Margaret Cavendish. Margaret was also a writer who published Poems and Fancies in 1653 and she was just as pissed as Aphra about her grave being in a place that didn't have much prestige.

Elwyn hadn't heard of Margaret Cavendish so he pointed out (in a tactful way) that Poets Corner was very exclusive, with writers like Charles Dickens being buried there. Margaret Cavendish said there were plenty of non-famous writers in Poets Corner who only got there because they were men.

Point taken, Elwyn said. He came up with a plan. He and the other Payne students would help the two dead female writers make a switch, tossing a couple of the not-as-important male writers out of their sepulchers, if they would let the group escape along the North transept near where the roof collapsed from a bomb during World War Two.

Deal, Margaret said and Aphra agreed. So the students went off to Poets Corner and started throwing moldy pillows and coffins around, rearranging the graves, with Margaret and Aphra keeping watch. The two dead women overheard someone ask Elwyn about his essay, and since they were both writers they wanted to know what it was.

"Meta-narrative." Janet finished her drink. "You have to give him points for that."

Fitger asked if there was more gin in the mini-fridge. "And how about a snack? Maybe some nuts?"

"I'll take a look." Janet opened the little cabinet. "There's one more gin. And they have cashews—but they're lightly salted. Aren't you supposed to avoid salt? I suppose I could rinse them."

"You can't rinse cashews," Fitger said.

She tossed him the package and opened another mini-bottle of gin.

Knee-deep in a skeleton, Elwyn told Aphra and Margaret about his assignment, that he was supposed to write about an experience he had in England. Whatever he wrote was sup-posed to be informative but also personal and original like the essays by James Baldwin and Joan Didion they read in class. And his professor (who was in the hospital) said he was not allowed to use the word "literally" unless he looked it up again and was sure he understood what it meant.

Aphra said she hadn't heard of the authors he mentioned but she was intrigued. And Margaret Cavendish, who some people insultingly called "Mad Madge," took a centuries-old quill pen from her ribcage and said What do you think, Aphra? Aphra shrugged, a shoulder bone coming out of its socket, and said, Okay, I haven't written anything good since Oroonoko.

"That's a good line," Fitger said. He was struggling to open the packet of cashews, salted nuts eventually spilling across the bed.

Elwyn gave Aphra Behn a notebook he had in his pocket and she got to work. Margaret Cavendish said, I will take care of the escape route, and on the way I will give Neville Chamberlain (haha literally, I think that is correct) a piece of my mind.

When Aphra's and Margaret's new sepulchers were almost ready, Aphra gave Elwyn his notebook. She said, This is a rough draft so you will have to rewrite it in your own style and FYI I included myself and Margaret Cavendish in it, I hope that's okay.

Elwyn said that it was.

Aphra and Margaret kept their promise and opened the North Door and Elwyn asked Aphra why she had helped him.

I could see something different in you, she said. I could see you had a great imagination.

Thanks, said Elwyn.

And you have a thick skin.

Haha, not funny, Elwyn said.

She apologized. If I was your professor, I would give you an A on your essay, she told him. It's definitely original. And it is obvious you worked hard and did all the assignments and learned something about England and also about yourself, which is probably supposed to be the point of the class.

Elwyn agreed. And he finished his essay, and the next day before he got on the plane he turned it in.

The End

"I'm not sure how you'll grade that," Janet said, "but I loved it. It was sweet, somehow, despite all the gore."

"Sweet" wasn't the word Fitger would have used to describe anything Elwyn had written but he didn't bother to disagree. He was plucking cashews out of the bedclothes. Janet finished

200

her drink and tossed her empty cup in the trash. "Were you planning to thank me, by the way? For coming to rescue you in England?"

"I thanked you," he said. "I'm sure I did."

"No. Wrong." Janet said she needed to go make her phone calls. "I'll see you at seven a.m. in the lobby?"

"I definitely thanked you," Fitger said.

She disagreed. When the door closed behind her, he turned out the light and lay in the dark. He was sure he had thanked her. Either way, it was something they could talk about again, the next day on the plane.

TWELVE

FINAL ESSAY FOR PROFESSOR FITGER

I AM STILL TRYING TO THINK OF A TITLE

It will be complicated
I think
to write an essay in the form of a poem
but that is what I am going to do because
I have always found it easier
to put my feelings into
verse.

Besides which
(this is a note for Professor Fitger, I hope you are ok)
you told us that our writing style
was like our fingerprint
and I think my style is more original
and creative
when I can express myself in the form
of a poem.

I will be focusing in this poem-essay
on Kensington Gardens
a place we visited as a group
but I came back to it later
after our professor got taken away to a hospital.
We had to pack to go home,
but I was mostly finished and I needed to be
out of
the dorm.

My first stop at Kensington Gardens
was the Albert Memorial.
Albert was the husband of
Queen Victoria
and you can see that she loved him
and missed him after he died
because of the statue.
There are steps leading up to it
and a big cement patio all around
and in the center, Albert
is protected from the rain
by a stone archway
maybe you would call it a shrine (though
I am not sure what the definition of a shrine really is).

I was looking at the quote on the Albert statue
where it says, "For a Life Devoted to the Public Good"
and then I heard someone call my name.
When I turned around I saw Elwyn
who was kind of a friend,

he went to the Kit-Cat Café with me
and now he was walking toward me
along the path.

The trees in Kensington Garden
are huge. Someone is definitely
taking care of them. I don't know what kind they are
because the British trees are different
from ours.
Besides, in winter, most of them
don't have leaves and look alike.
I told Elwyn that
in the summer, I imagined
they would look like big pieces
of broccoli.

We walked down the path.
It was a hard sad day
with our professor being in the hospital
and I had suffered a loss
that I will describe
in the second half of this poem.
Eventually
Elwyn and I came to the Princess Diana
Memorial Fountain.
Princess Diana was married for a while
to Charles and maybe could have been queen,
but they got divorced and
Diana died in a car crash with a man

she was dating. I don't know
much about Diana because everything happened to her
before I was born.

The memorial is a fountain
in the shape of a circle
like the letter O
with the water running
around and around.
It isn't deep
but parts of the circle
are steeper or faster
than others.
We watched the water going around
and Elwyn was really nice
He said he followed me from the dorm because he
could tell that
I was upset.

Well that was the straw of the camel
because
I was already sad about the Loss
that I mentioned earlier in this poem
and about our professor being in the hospital.
Elwyn gave me a tissue and
we sat down near some geese.
They were pecking at something
Maybe worms or bugs
in the grass.

After a while Elwyn asked
if I had written my final assignment
I said no
I was having trouble with it because
I only wanted to write
about my cat, Mrs. Gray.

Elwyn knew I liked poems
(I showed him one)
and he said
if I wanted to write about Mrs. Gray
and about the Princess Diana Memorial Fountain
with everything rolled together
into a poem
I should just go ahead.
I told Elwyn that I would
give it a try.

PART TWO:
Let me start this second half of my poem
by saying that
I have never known another cat
like Mrs. Gray.
Her fur was not just soft,
it was thick and fine
like chinchilla fur.
She even had tufts of fur
on the bottoms of her paws.
Her meow
was like a musical question mark

always polite
She was the most charming and
the smartest cat that has ever lived.

My mother didn't want to tell me at first
that my pet had died. She wanted to wait
until I got home.
But I knew when she called me
that something was wrong.
Mrs. Gray died in my bedroom.
My mother said
she hadn't kept her kibble down
and she (my mother) was planning to take her to the vet
but then she found her in my room.
Mrs. Gray
had crawled up onto my bed
and died on my pillow.
My mother and I both cried on the phone.

Now I will back up
like in a flashback.
Mrs. Gray has been a part of my life
since I was three years old.
I went with my mother
to the farmer's market
and we saw a teenage boy with four fluffy kittens
in a cardboard box.
My mother said I could choose one
and I chose the one that was sitting
by herself

with wide green eyes.
My mother suggested we could call her Fluff
but I insisted on
Mrs. Gray.

I fed her every day
and brushed her.
She always came when I called
I sometimes dressed her in doll clothes
She was so patient
She used to wait for me
in the front window
when I got home from school.

I am not doing her justice
but the point is, she was
exceptional
and I know you told us that 'very unique'
is not correct
but that's what she was.

We were still sitting
next to the Princess Diana Memorial fountain
and Elwyn pointed out the words
sculpted into the stone
that said
Opened by Her Majesty the Queen on 6th July 2004
July 6 is my birthday
I told this to Elwyn and we both thought about it
while the geese and a black bird with yellow legs

like a witch's stockings
walked to the fountain's opposite side.

Elwyn actually
knew a lot about Princess Diana
He told me her last words
after the car crash that killed her were
"My god, what's happened?"
which I guess is what you would say right after
a terrible accident.
That made me think about Mrs. Gray again.
I can't believe she is gone.
She was the animal of my heart.

When I get home
I am going to put a marker in the front yard
of my house
near the front stoop
by the rhododendron bush where Mrs. Gray liked to sit
underneath the flowers in the spring
and whenever I see the marker I will think
about Mrs. Gray
but maybe also sometimes about Princess Diana
and about her fountain
with the water running around and around it
like a circle of grief.

Professor Fitger, I hope you are okay
and I hope if you read this
you will forgive

some of the bad handwriting
in this poem but
the printer in the dorm wasn't working.
I did write a first draft but Sonia
told me
the printer had stopped working
so I had to copy it all out
like this
and my hand is tired.

Before I finish
I want to thank you
for this class
which has been an experience
just like the title said.
I also want to say
that I think you are a really good professor
even if your score on
Rate my professor
is not very high.

At the Princess Diana fountain it had started to rain
so Elwyn and I took the Underground
to the dorm.

That brings me back
full circle I guess
to Mrs. Gray
who by now you know
was more than a cat to me

or a pet.
I loved her so much.

Well,
I have written my heart out
as best I can
in this poem.
Please let me know
how I can get it back.
It is the only copy
I have.

"Janet! There you are!" Fitger waved to her when he saw her wheeling her suitcase into the lobby. He had woken up early and ordered breakfast in the café downstairs. He gestured to the cup of fruit salad on the table in front of him and told her he had saved it especially for her. "Come sit," he said.

"I'm not hungry." She looked disheveled; her hair was oddly flat on one side. She parked her suitcase next to his and said she was going to the desk to check out.

"No need to rush. What do you suppose I've been doing?" Fitger asked.

Janet said she wasn't in the mood to play twenty questions.

"I'll give you the answer, then. Look." He gestured toward the morning paper and the student essays that were scattered across the table with the remains of his breakfast. "The dizziness: I woke up and it was gone. I've been sitting here reading." He picked up Felicity's poem and held it out so Janet could see it. "The demise of a feline, in verse." He had prohibited the use of poetic forms, he explained, but in light of his absence at the end of the term, and given the liberties some of the other students had taken in their final assignments, a penalty in this instance would hardly seem fair. As a poem, Felicity's still-untitled opus was undistinguished, and yet while reading it, eyesight restored and with a cup of lukewarm coffee beside him, he had felt almost . . . moved.

Janet was clearly not paying attention. Muttering something about calling a cab, she dragged her suitcase—one of the wheels was catawampus—to the hotel desk. Fitger gathered up his belongings and met her a few minutes later out on the sidewalk. Her bland reaction to his recovery struck him as strange. "Are you feeling all right?" he asked.

Yes, Janet said. She had a headache. Otherwise, she was fine.

Fitger wondered aloud if her headache had been caused by the gin. Or it could be the preflight stress. Or lack of sleep. She was usually an early riser, but he had been waiting for her in the lobby rather than vice versa. Which was fine; he didn't mind. But she did look a bit tired. In fact, she looked—

"What?" she snapped, wheeling around to face him. "I look like *what?*"

"Nothing," he said. "I mean, you look fine."

"Good." She asked if he was wearing his compression socks. He was.

They got separated at Heathrow, Fitger being categorized as a less desirable sort of traveler and shunted to the longest of the check-in lines. On his way to the gate, he sent Janet a text—*meet for coffee?*—but she didn't reply. Well, he would talk to her soon, on the plane. At a newsstand, he spent the last of his British pounds on a packet of chocolates and a novel—a book he'd read about when it won an international prize. Shoving it into his carry-on bag, he felt buoyant, almost lighthearted. He was a sinner whose sins had been pardoned: everything in the airport was fully in focus—timetables, advertisements, the T-shirts of his fellow travelers. A miracle: he could read.

When he boarded the plane, he found Janet already seated, her face partly covered with a sleeping mask. Their seats were together; she'd taken the aisle. He climbed over her knees and wedged himself between two metal armrests. *Ah, England,* he thought. Now that he was leaving, he felt a bemused affection for all things British, despite the lack of good food and the rain.

Soon the plane was rolling down the runway and hefting its body into the air. Janet took off her sleep mask and began to fiddle with the video screen in the facing seat back, scrolling through in-flight movie options. She had a preference for crime dramas of the bloodthirsty kind.

Fitger offered her a chocolate. "How's your headache?" he asked.

She waved the chocolates away and said she didn't want to talk. "I'm going to watch a movie. Did they bring us headphones?"

"No. Maybe they'll hand them out with the food." Fitger watched as she queued up a film—something brutal and thuggish.

"Dammit. I must have packed mine in my suitcase," Janet

said. "They should hand out headphones as soon as we board." She began rifling, somewhat desperately, Fitger thought, through the belongings in her seat-back pocket: an iPad, a toothbrush and hairbrush, a scarf, a magazine, and a plastic container of food with sub-units for almonds, dried fruit, and cheese.

"You're like a chipmunk in a burrow over there," he said. "May I say just one thing about our conversation last night?"

"No." She pressed the flight attendant call-button.

"You know I never owned a dog before. And though my behavior toward Rogaine hasn't been lavish or devoted, I—"

Janet lurched up out of her seat and headed toward the front of the plane, Fitger wondering if she was going to demand to fly it. A few minutes later, when she returned, she was tearing open a package of earphones with her teeth. "Here." She tossed a second package into his lap. "I'm going to watch a movie. I don't want to talk." She suggested that Fitger take advantage of his lack of vertigo to choose his own film or start reading his book.

Fine. Putting a pillow behind him—airline seats, he had always believed, were designed for hunchbacks—Fitger examined the cover of the novel he had bought at the newsstand. It bore multiple rapturous stamps of endorsement, presumably from the author's inner circle of friends. He read the copyright page and the acknowledgments and the dedication. To his left, a middle-aged couple was whispering and giggling under a blanket. To his right, Janet was watching one thug beating another to death with a baseball bat in a parking garage.

Twenty pages into the prizewinning book, Fitger found

the plot predictable and the prose bloated with quirks and pretentions. He flipped to the end: the final pages confirmed this impression. He stuffed the novel into his seat-back pocket. The couple to his left was kissing, the woman's eyes briefly meeting Fitger's over her partner's head. He turned away, eating some of his chocolates and swiveling his ankles, to ward off blood clots. Six more hours until they landed. He reached for the folder of student essays, planning to grade and dispose of them once and for all.

BRENT SCHRAFT

OUTLINE DRAFT OF MY FINAL ESSAY FOR PROFESSOR FITGER'S JANUARY TERM CLASS IN ENGLAND

(This is still a rough draft because Professor Fitger said he would help me after I wrote my first version as an outline but then he cracked his head on a stone. Whoever is grading this let me know when I will have to revise and turn it back in.)

The sections of the outline/draft that followed included "The Place I am Describing and the Reasons I Picked It" and "My Evidence for What I am Saying."

I am not a good writer even though I had to take freshman writing twice. And the second time my instructor spoke with a foreign accent and he still understood American grammar better than me. Well we can't all be good at the same thing and I am better at math. I want to say here that I am trying, I have worked hard in this class I am not just biting my time. Also I am partly deaf in one ear due to a childhood illness that doesn't make anything easier where I am concerned.

"Come on, Brent," Fitger murmured. "I'd actually like to give you a C." The topic of the essay was, ostensibly, a chalkboard in Oxford's Museum of the History of Science, which was started by a man named Ashmole a name he must of hated, I should know because in high school people turned my name Brent Schraft into Bent Shaft.

The essay went on to describe the chalkboard, which hung on a wall in the museum's basement and bore the writing of Albert Einstein, who had been calculating—during a lecture—the size of the universe. (Einstein was incredibly smart. He probably would have gone to a college like Oxford instead of Payne.) Fitger remembered seeing Brent standing open-mouthed in front of the chalkboard with its calculations. (I am good at math but not good enough I guess because I didn't understand what he wrote. Even if I studied a long time I don't think that I could.) Brent included a photo of the chalkboard. The rest of his essay bumbled into rabbit holes and blind alleys, Brent hunting for meaning and connections and synonyms (I can't think of another word for 'anyway' nothing else is the same) and careening toward a sudden conclusion which involved Sonia not wanting to give him a blow job (I was always willing to go down on her) and a plea that Fitger, alone, be in charge of his grade. (He understands how I struggle and taught me a lot about failure because he has screwed up his life too but you try to keep going.)

Janet unplugged herself from her earbuds and tied them ferociously into a knot. "This pair is crap. I had the volume turned all the way up, and I could still barely hear."

Fitger was rereading Brent's conclusion: because he has screwed up his life too but you try to keep going. A valid and admirable point; and Fitger hoped that his students, with whom he was seldom in touch when a class was finished, would persevere and be well and succeed. Had he read all their papers? Here were the final compositions from Sonia, Joe, Wyatt, D.B., Lin, the twins, Elwyn, Felicity, and Brent.

Counting the twins as two, that was ten. One was missing. *Xanna.* Damn. She had wanted to write about the London Eye. "One of the assignments isn't here," he told Janet, as the plane, encountering "rough air," appeared to skip like a rock on a pond. "Do you have it?"

"Why would I have it?"

Some sort of meal was trundling toward them on a metal cart. Janet reached for her personal Tupperware picnic—she didn't eat airline food—and lowered her tray.

Fitger counted the essays again. "How many did you originally collect at the airport?"

"I didn't count them."

"But I thought you—"

"And do you want to know *why* I didn't count them?" The cords on her neck, Fitger noticed, were taut like the cables on a suspension bridge. "Because I had just flown to England on virtually no notice, and spent the night packing up the dirty laundry in your room and booking a train ticket to Bath so I could visit you in a hospital. And then, on about three hours' sleep, I had to wake your students up and get them to the airport. So I don't remember how many essays I collected." She turned the latch on the seatback in front of him, and a plastic tray table flopped into his lap. Something orange and sticky coated its surface.

Xanna Blythe, Fitger thought. What a mess he had made. If she didn't finish the class it would haunt him.

Janet had requisitioned his earbuds and inserted them into her ears.

Fitger clambered over her lap and into the aisle, returning

218

from the lavatory with a wad of paper towels that dripped from his hands.

"Squeeze those out," Janet said. "They're too wet."

Fitger squeezed out the towels.

"Sir?" The food cart had reached the row in front of them, and the nearest flight attendant said she would appreciate it if he didn't drip his way through the plane's narrow aisle. Had he not been given a wet wipe before takeoff?

Yes, Fitger said, but he had used his airline-provided wipe to clean his hands, not realizing that he would be in charge of janitorial work for his region.

The plane dipped and then rose, and an announcement over the intercom asked everyone to return to their seats. Janet let Fitger pass. He clicked his table into its upright position and watched the meal cart rattle away.

Janet was eating her cubes of white cheese. He liked watching her eat; she held her hands close to her face, like a squirrel. "I know you don't want to talk to me," he said. "But I'm sure you can hear me, because those earphones are terrible. It doesn't matter which pair you use."

On the screen in front of her, one man was removing another's fingers with garden shears.

"I'm not going to follow you to Chicago," Fitger said. "I don't want you to think of me as a pest. Of course, I *am* sometimes a pest—but that's not my intent."

The plane shuddered, and the pilot made an announcement about "more bumps ahead."

"Rogaine would choose you, I'm sure, if we gave him the choice between us. You're the one who thought to adopt him,"

Fitger said. In the film Janet was watching, a severed finger rolled off the edge of a table and onto the ground. "He was probably on a euthanasia list at that final shelter, the one where he spent his formative years—that Misfit Farm."

"*Mission* Farm," Janet said.

The plane dropped, then lifted, and their hands met on the armrest between them, Fitger remembering the dampness of the stone where he had fallen after he left the Roman Baths, the ring of student faces above and the near-asphyxiating pain in his chest, the highway of lightning in his left arm.

A static-filled message emerged from the plane's speakers. "I want you to take the dog," Fitger said.

He waited while she took a deep breath. When she pulled out her earbuds, he repeated himself in case she hadn't heard. "I cede my half of him," he said. "You won't want to come home to a new place at the end of the day and be alone. Rogaine is old and set in his ways; he would grieve if you left him behind. And I'm sure you can hire a dog-walker—someone who doesn't mind being bitten now and then."

"Are you only saying that because you think we're going to die in a plane crash?" Janet asked.

"No. We're not going to crash. I already had my near-death experience."

The plane swerved horizontally, as if swept to the side by a giant hand.

"Jay, we don't have to—"

"Wait," he said. "My only request is that you bring him along if you come back to Payne to visit. Of course, if I get a highly paid position elsewhere, or have the sense to retire, I could end up moving to—"

"They rescinded the offer," Janet said.

"What?" A second garbled announcement was piped through the speakers.

"They rescinded it," she said. "Last night on the phone. So I won't be moving to Chicago."

"But you already accepted the job," Fitger said.

"I accepted it over the phone. But I hadn't signed. The committee chair called me with the 'unhappy news.' Budget cuts, he said. Very sudden and unexpected."

"That sounds like embezzlement," Fitger murmured. "Or some sort of malfeasance. Can you appeal?"

She shook her head. "I didn't sign. I was hoping for a better salary."

One of the overhead bins opened and spilled its contents, a sweatshirt landing at Janet's feet.

"I suppose . . . you could apply somewhere else," Fitger said. He held his breath; hope sluiced through the crimson knob of his heart.

Janet nodded and said maybe she would. "But you can't leave or retire, Jay. You would be lost without Payne. That place is a part of you. It's in your bones."

Was it? Was Payne in his bones?

A few cans of soda rolled down the aisle. "I guess I should thank you for coming to rescue me," Fitger said. "Unless I did that already."

Janet plugged in her earbuds. There were five hours left of their flight, she said, and if they survived—if she didn't kill him—it would be his turn to pick up the dog when they got home.

THIRTEEN

XANNA BLYTHE
FINAL (LATE) PAPER, THE ENGLISH EXPERIENCE

Dear Professor Fitger:

You've probably forgotten about me by now; I was in your Experience: England class three years ago. I never turned in my final paper and you gave me a semester grade of "I" for incomplete, even though I could have finished with a B-minus, and even though the policy on your syllabus said that incompletes were by permission only, after written request.

I never requested the incomplete.

I'm not sure what your wife or girlfriend or whatever told you, but I actually did write my essay—the one about the London Eye. I had it in my hand when she met us at the airport, but when everyone else was turning theirs in I threw mine in the trash. My high school guidance counselor, Ms. Forster, would have chalked that up to my "tendency to self-sabotage." (A weird correspondence: lupus—because it attacks the immune system—is also a form of self-sabotage. Mine's mostly under control these days, thanks for asking. I shaved my head again [hair loss] and got some new meds.)

What have I been doing with my life these past three years? Avoiding the question of what to do with my life and working retail. When I wasn't picking clothes off the floor of a dressing room, I took classes online. I took thirty-two credits but I still couldn't get my Payne diploma, because the registrar's office told me I had to take care of my incomplete. I had enough credits for graduation but the incomplete was like a hole in my transcript and it had to be filled.

Anyway: I got the emails you sent me when you got back to Payne, but by then I'd already left campus. I know you apologized for calling me a liar about needing to rest when I felt sick, and you told me I could turn in whatever I'd written even if my essay wasn't finished, but, hey, I was pissed.

Full disclosure: I wasn't happy with what I'd written, which is part of the reason why I threw it away. I wanted to write something that would impress you, and I had what I thought was a great idea, which was writing my paper in the form of a Ferris wheel, with thirty-two separate parts or pods (the London Eye has thirty-two pods, but they're numbered one to thirty-three, because triskaidekaphobes are afraid of the number 13.) I got the idea one day during class while we were in England, when you went on a rant about endings. You said an ending in an essay should feel like a door that swings shut— but the writer should leave a crack of light around the frame so people would wonder what might exist, on the other side.

That made me think about the London Eye, because I wanted to write a different kind of essay, maybe something that went around in a circle and didn't end. I kept thinking about a many-spoked creature with all kinds of tangents and offshoots, little containers of thought spinning slowly around. But I couldn't get it in the right order, and while we were waiting to go through security and everybody was asking your girlfriend (or maybe wife) if she had heard anything from the hospital, I looked at my paper and knew it didn't work the way that I wanted. There was no crack of light like the one you described. There was something about the London Eye that I really loved but I didn't know how to explain what it was.

(Speaking of explaining: I should probably let you know that if some of the other students' essays from that term were kind of weird, that's because I told them that I'd taken a class with you before and you gave the best grades to projects that were experimental.)

At home, after I left campus, my mother asked me approximately ten thousand times about finishing your class. Why didn't I finish? My professor hadn't really meant what he'd said; he probably forgot about the lupus; he'd apologized and sent such a nice note. Couldn't I just describe that giant merry-go-round or whatever it was, now that he'd promised he would still accept my paper no matter how late I turned it in?

For some reason I couldn't.

The amount of time I've spent thinking about the London Eye is absurd.

Here's something you might not have expected: the students from our class have all stayed in touch. Felicity made us a Facebook group after we went through security (we were kind of a mess; somebody mentioned the idea that teaching our class had killed you) on our way back to Payne. I don't think anyone accessed the group very much at first but we knew it was there.

Felicity has a job at Payne now, working in admissions. She posted about it a few months ago and said she's happy. She has her own apartment, and she got a new cat named Mr.

Brown. When she posted about the job and included a picture of her new cat she asked the rest of us what we were up to, and people gradually answered. The twins are living in London. They love it, they got some kind of artist fellowship. Cass says they're hoping to stay there forever and never come home.

Joe Ballo is working at a restaurant in Iowa City. He's saving money so he can go to seminary school.

I made the mistake of letting people know that I still hadn't turned in my final essay, and some of them have given me shit ever since. Lin asked me what it was about and I said I wasn't sure, because it was about a lot of different things or maybe nothing, and she said, Cool because that would make it easy to finish. She started emailing me every week. *Three years?!* She finally threatened to write the essay for me if I wouldn't write it myself, but I told her I didn't want her violating a legal code before she passed the bar. She's in her second year of law school in California, specializing in immigration law.

In case you're curious: I rode the London Eye twice while we were in England; the second time in the dark. When you're at the top, the buildings and bridges along the Thames look like bright little toys.

I know I'm not the only one from our class who dropped out. Brent had a hard time. But even he gave me shit about not turning in my final essay. He told me he remembered one day in class when I asked a question and you said that I needed to trust my intelligence. I'd forgotten about that. Brent said he was jealous because you said I had "interesting thoughts." I guess he's getting his degree next month from a community college. He stopped interacting with the Facebook group when Sonia announced that she was getting married. She wants to study social work. She posted a picture of herself with her fiancé—a woman who had cancer and lost a leg below the knee.

Elwyn posted a picture, too—he looks happy. He has a girlfriend and lives in Wisconsin. He said they met when they were both working at a haunted house, out in a cornfield, at Halloween.

D.B.'s only post said he's working "in the security field." Lin says that probably means CIA.

The last time Lin nagged me about my essay I told her I wanted to write about the London Eye, but not really talk about the Eye at all; I wanted to write about the inside of my head and about other things that I couldn't describe. Like wanting to be good at something and being afraid you never will. And I also wanted to write about endings, because you always said they were hard. And also perspective—seeing things from different angles, and in different lights. I hope I have more perspective now than I did when I was nineteen.

Lin reminded me that you used to talk about including the struggle to write in our writing. And she gave me a deadline. Lin and I didn't like each other much when we were in England but now we seem to be friends.

Wyatt's an EMT; he got his license. He lives in Colorado and says he goes hiking up in the mountains almost every weekend. He said he gave up the drugs and the drinking and he's in a support group. In the photo he sent, he's holding a baby. He helped deliver it when the parents' car slid off the road on the way to a hospital and got stuck in snow. You should see the expression on his face in the picture, his eyes wide open, holding that baby wrapped in a blanket. It was a girl, but the parents gave it Wyatt as a middle name.

I know it seems like I'm not writing about the London Eye, but in some way I am. What I liked about being up there was being able to see.

I'm sorry this is three and a half years overdue. After I printed it out I panicked, thinking that maybe it would be too late, after all, to hand it in. So I drove here, four hours to campus (I'm going to stay overnight with Felicity), feeling like I was traveling back in time and wondering what I would do if you had left Payne, if you had taken a different job or retired. But then I walked across the quad and saw you coming down the steps of Willard Hall with your wife or girlfriend, the one from the airport, and the two of you were walking a puppy on a leash. I didn't know you liked dogs.

Thanks for the English Experience. I'm putting a copy of this paper under your door.

Acknowledgments

Thank you, thank you to my wonderful agent, Henry Dunow, and to the equally wonderful Lee Boudreaux and Cara Reilly at Doubleday. To the peerless Michael Goldsmith and the indomitable Jason Gobble, I remain deeply indebted, as per usual, and I am grateful to Anne Jaconette for her savvy and her expertise. Gerald Howard: thanks for being the first to publish Professor Fitger. Emily Mahon, Betty Lew, and Evan Sklar: you made this book and its cover lovely. Nora Reichard: thanks for weeding those errors out of my prose.

To my dear friend and reader Alison McGhee, eternal thanks—what would I do without you? To Daniel Bruggeman, thank you so much for turning the Wagner-Hall twins into talented artists and for giving them a physical form.

I'm very grateful to my colleagues in the Creative Writing Program at the University of Minnesota and, in particular, to Charles Baxter and Patricia Hampl, who offered insight and advice along the way. Brent Latchaw, Rachel Drake, Jessica McKenna, Nanette Hanks, and Martha Johnson offered much-needed travel-abroad wisdom and help with administrative snags.

Sincere thanks to Lindsey Lahr and the Learning Abroad

Center at the University of Minnesota, and to Yukiko Okazaki at the Fundación José Ortega y Gasset/Gregorio Marañón in Toledo, Spain; I'll be back.

My gratitude to Desmond King at Nuffield College in Oxford, U.K.: Professor Fitger wouldn't have gone to England without you.

Thanks and love, as always, to Lawrence Jacobs. We met more than forty years ago in freshman English and have had so many adventures since.

To Emma and Isabella: I love you both. And to Bika Ruth Jacobs: let me know what you think of this book when you are old enough to read.

About the Author

Julie Schumacher grew up in Wilmington, Delaware, and graduated from Oberlin College and Cornell University, where she earned her MFA. Her first novel, *The Body Is Water,* was an ALA Notable Book of the Year and a finalist for the PEN/Hemingway Award. Her 2014 novel, *Dear Committee Members,* won the Thurber Prize for American Humor; she is the first woman to have been so honored. She lives in St. Paul and is a faculty member in the Creative Writing Program and the Department of English at the University of Minnesota.